PARAGON - THE BLACK DOG

WHITNEY J COGLE

MOCHAFROG
Publishing

WHITNEY J. COGLE

PARAGON
THE BLACK DOG

DEDICATION

To my girls who used to pray every night that "Momma would get her books published." Thank you for making it as big a deal in your life as it is in mine!

PROLOGUE

Makk sat in a dark tunnel in an upright fetal position, barefoot and cold, yet he could feel beads of sweat on his bulbous, hairless head. He glanced down at his long-fingered hand where he held his treasure. Since finding the magical stone, it had mesmerized him. It lay in his palm like a misshapen, ruby-colored marble, glittering as he shined his flashlight upon it. Never had he seen anything so beautiful. Well, he'd been able to accurately say that before he'd met her, the queen. By the Earth's core, she was lovely. The most amazing creature ever created.

Makk had gifted both the queen and his sister a chunk of his precious stone, which they'd gladly accepted, abandoning him to make their home on the outside. He rolled his eyes upward, banging the back of his head painfully against the rock behind him, hoping he hadn't made a mistake. But he was sure he had. Giving them the stones was the reason he was alone now. It had changed everything.

"I know you're out there somewhere," he whispered. How he longed to be with the queen above ground, but it was dangerous—at least for someone as freakish as him. Not only would he not fit in, but the sun would burn him alive. He would never survive it.

At one time, Makk had only known one emotion. Rend, the Unit Guard who would come and check on him from time to time called it being "sad." Regardless of its name, he didn't like it. He felt it now as he contemplated what once was—his family that was no more. He'd always felt the sad feeling or nothing at all until the stone came into his life. It seemed to awaken other emotions within him, ones he didn't even know existed.

Rend had brought him books that the foragers had found. "Up there." He looked up. Makk had never been on the outside. Rend said it wasn't safe. He called the beings that lived there "people" sometimes, but mostly he called them "beasts" or "killers." Makk didn't know what people looked like, but if they were beasts or killers, he didn't want any part of them.

He put his stone to the side and picked up his favorite book of poems written by an outsider named Oscar Wilde. One poem, titled *Her Voice,* was his favorite.

> And there is nothing left to do
> But to kill once again, and part.
> Nay, there is nothing we should rue,
> I have my beauty, - you your Art,
> Nay, do not start,
> One world was not enough for two
> Like me and you.

He sighed deeply, loving the sound of the words, even though he didn't understand some of them. He grabbed the dictionary Rend had given him and looked up rue. "Regret or sorrow," he said aloud. This word described his situation perfectly. He regretted letting the queen go and he was filled with sorrow.

The day she stepped into their lives was seared into his memory. She'd taken their empty, joyless existence and filled it with something real. Something magical. She'd given them something to look forward to, and that something was her.

The queen had been gone for years now. No matter. She would never love him any more than she would love a brother. "How could she love someone so ugly?" He was very much aware of his repulsiveness. He'd seen his reflection in a piece of a mirror he'd found and understood he was no match for her perfection.

If only he could have the queen back, just so he could look at her every day. That's all he wanted—just to see her.

Out of the darkness, crimson glowed into his eyelids. It was the stone glowing a soft red beside him. His small mouth opened as he gazed upon its splendor. Soon, the light flickered out and died. Yet, its afterglow lingered, leaving his heart lighter, like the stone helped him somehow.

What did this mean? Was it a sign? For an extensive time, he stared at his amazing gem, waiting for it to light up again, but it did not. He was so obsessed that he didn't even want to dig, even though that was his second favorite thing to do besides reading. The queen had been the only one who could make the stone glow. Now here he was doing it himself! It was a miracle.

After a long time passed, and the stone remained dark, he grabbed his dictionary again. He liked to learn new words, marking each with an underline. Opening it at random, he ran his grayish finger down the page until he came upon a word that he'd never read before.

"Paragon. A person or thing that is perfect or excellent in some way." That word described the stone exactly, and it also described the beautiful queen. "That's what you are. Just like her." He picked it up and held it close to his face.

"Paragon."

PART I

SOMETHING IS
WATCHING

1

SIX MONTHS AGO…

It was late when the three boys took off through the woods on a dare. Brian and his cousin Thad darted through the almost bare trees, leaving Jay trailing behind. The moon was full and bright, casting a blue glow upon the darkness. It was eerily silent. No crickets chirped, no birds sang, no creatures moved. The air was unusually damp and smelled fresh as the dead leaves crunched loudly beneath his shoes, violently breaking the silence.

Their pace slowed as they arrived at their destination. When Jay caught up, the three of them scrambled through the barbed-wire fence. Jay's breathing grew shallow as he anticipated what he might see, grateful that at least he was the only one in the group not guilty of trespassing. A sudden breeze overtook him, provoking him to close his jacket tight against it as the leaves danced around his feet. Despite the chilly air, a bead of sweat dripped from underneath his Rockies cap into his eye.

"Let's go, wimp," Brian barked at Jay when he hesitated. "It's not a big deal. Move it!"

Some kids at school said this place was haunted. Brian and Thad, who were starting to develop a reputation of being bullies had insisted those were just rumors started by some wussy losers who'd never even been there. Jay's skin crawled at the thought, and he didn't want to know. To know would be too painful, too weird, too wrong. Still there he was, against his will, doing exactly what he was told, as always.

A structure appeared through the woods out of nowhere, stopping them in their tracks—a shell of a house burnt down to almost nothing, black and charred. Naked trees with their crooked branches seemed to reach out for it like malformed skeletons.

The house at one time had been beautiful, filled with love, laughter, and happiness. Stories were read, dinners cooked, games played. Now all that remained was blackness and soot. All except for a trellis that shone white in the moonlight and had several vines growing through its lattice sides. It was the one thing that hadn't been destroyed. As a matter of fact, it seemed untouched. Memories shot through Jay's mind at the sight. In front of it materialized a family, making his heart ache as he admired them through watery eyes.

Jay lost his breath as a white light caught his eye glowing from the corner of the thing that used to be a home. A sad voice along with a female crying accompanied it—quiet at first. Chills ran up and down his body.

"No-o-o!" The voice screamed out in an eerie, deathly piercing sound, silencing his heart within his chest. The three boys ducked behind some shrubbery and watched with dread as a woman's head and torso appeared out of the rubble. Both her hair and clothing were of the same bright white, shining like a beacon in the soft light that surrounded her. An unseen child begged her to be quiet, but the woman wouldn't listen.

"No! Please! This can't be!" The agony in her voice was almost too much to tolerate. Was it the residual energy of pain felt long ago? Was it her? Could it be the one who'd died there? No, it couldn't be. Jay recalled she had been young when she'd died, and this woman appeared old.

Two figures, oddly shaped with long arms and legs emerged, each grabbing the lady on opposite sides as she screamed all the louder, "No!"

"What are those things?" Thad whispered with a shake in his voice, his question met with heavy breathing, bringing with it puffs of steam in the frosty air.

Although difficult to make out in the shadows, the creatures were dark, not normal. A red light began to take over and engulfed the woman and the two things by her side, as if hell itself had opened and was trying to swallow them.

The boys scrambled and Brian whispered, "Let's go!"

Jay stood fast, powerless to move his shaky legs, unable to take his eyes off what he was seeing. He'd realized his friends had deserted him, and yet it didn't seem to matter all that much. He knew he should follow them out of there, but he couldn't. It seemed he was watching a battle of spirits and he wanted to see what would happen next. He had to.

The urge to rescue the poor angel consumed him, but he was no match. All he could do was watch with helplessness as the demons dragged the beautiful spirit downward, away from view as she screamed in painful desperation. The sound of it seemed to tear through his soul. Then the light disappeared as quickly as it had come, leaving Jay alone in the darkness.

A soft wind blew, stirring up the dead leaves around him and everything was as silent as before the woman had made her appearance—as if it hadn't happened at all. The only thing that remained as proof of the incident was the heavy beating of Jay's heart and a chilling, dark fear deep within his soul.

2

SIX MONTHS LATER...

The swinging door of the Humane Society flew open and Jay barged through, grinning when Miss Connie jumped from behind the counter. The stink of medicine, vitamins, and animal hair hit him hard. As strange as it sounded, he found comfort in the smell. It meant he was home.

"Hi, Jay," Miss Connie murmured after composing herself, a wrinkled hand on her chest.

"Hey, Miss Connie. Aunt Vicki in back?" Aunt Vicki made Jay call anyone over twenty "Miss" or "Mister" which was pretty annoying. And Miss Connie was way over twenty. She had to be at least a hundred.

She peered over glasses with her eyes only, probably not really seeing him, then back down to her paperwork. She was so short that her arms lying on the counter were equal in height with her shoulder blades. If her hands were at her sides, her grayish-blue-haired head would have appeared as if sitting on top of the counter like a morbid decoration. "Yup. Feeding the pooches," she said, still out of breath from the scare.

"'K." Jay headed to the back of the room where Aunt Vicki sat a bowl of water in front of a dirty, fuzzy, cream-colored dog, then gave it a loving pat.

"Such a good boy, yes you are," she cooed in baby talk. Jay shook his head. Sometimes it seemed Aunt Vicki loved the dogs and cats she took care of more than she loved people.

Except for his goldfish Sampson, who basically spent all day circling a plastic castle in his round glass bowl, Jay had never had a pet. Since Aunt Vicki moved into the guest house in their backyard to help him and Dad about twelve years ago after Mom had died, she'd instilled in him the love of animals. Although he didn't go so far as to become a strict vegan like her, she was a big influence in his life.

"Pets can be so therapeutic," Aunt Vicki told him one day when he was little. "No one can give you the love your mother did, Jay. You will always miss her. But loving and taking care of animals can take away the sting." She'd been totally right. Working with the animals had been like a Band-Aid, or at least like that spray stuff that makes the sore less painful.

"Hi, Aunt Vicki."

"Hi, baby doll." She smiled with adoration.

Hot blood rushed to his face. "Aunt Vicki, please." A girl cleaning the cages glanced his way and giggled into her hand. Her name was Kayla. Or maybe Kylie—something like that. She had long dark hair pulled into a high ponytail, and she wore a baby blue Humane Society t-shirt. She was legit hot, and Aunt Vicki was being so embarrassing. And yet, she was nothing next to Lydia— the girl that had been inside his brain since he met her about a year ago in ninth grade. No one was as hot as Lydia, and that was a simple fact.

"Sorry, hon. Old habits, you know. How's your day?" Aunt Vicki moved her straight, fine, light-brown, frosted hair out of her eyes with her forearm as she stood with her hip popped out and her weight on one petite leg. She placed a hand on her hip, her long, skinny fingers hanging off her side like a flesh-colored spider.

"Fine," he answered, a twinge of irritation still lingering in his tone.

"Take off that hat, wouldja?" She reached over and gently grabbed Jay's black Colorado Rockies cap that he wore every day off his head and handed it to him. She never liked him wearing it indoors, and he was so used to it being on his head that he would habitually forget.

"Sorry." He knelt on his knees in front of the new, scrawny looking dog and began petting it. Soon, Aunt Vicki joined him, doing the same. "When did this one come in?"

He studied her as she answered him. Though she was his mother's sister, she looked nothing like Mom's picture. She didn't look as old as she probably was either. She had no lines around her eyes like Dad had. Dad always said she hadn't aged a day since he'd known her. She gave the credit to her good skin genes whenever he'd mentioned it. That and not eating anything with a face.

"This morning. Cute, isn't he?" She scratched behind his ears as his eyes closed halfway with delight.

"Yeah. Is he a cockapoo?"

"Nice." Aunt Vicki seemed impressed. "You're getting pretty good at that."

Jay kept his focus on the dog, holding back a smile through tight lips.

"He was abused," she explained. "See how he ducks away every time you raise your hand?" She demonstrated by lifting her hand and sure enough his head bobbed down, anticipating a strike. The poor dog's fear broke Jay's heart. "Someone must have smacked him on a regular basis."

"Poor guy." Jay stroked his coarse fur, hoping to calm him.

"There sure are some real jerks out there. Some that shouldn't be permitted to roam the planet." She exhaled as if to rid herself of the mere thought. "So, anything exciting happen today?" she asked, slapping her knees that were covered by a navy-blue apron.

"No." As an afterthought, he said, "Just saw the dog again."

Aunt Vicki lifted her head, an odd expression on her face. She always acted strange when he brought it up. "The one with the blue eyes?"

Jay nodded.

"You've been seeing it a lot lately."

"Yeah, it's been showing up like pretty much every day. Right in the same spot on Mercy Lane after you round the corner from the cul-de-sac."

"Hmm." Aunt Vicki patted the cockapoo's head, appearing to be deep in thought.

"You should see it. It's so weird with its black fur and bright blue eyes."

Aunt Vicki ticked her head. "That combo is pretty rare."

"The eyes look like they could almost glow in the dark. And it peeks at me from behind the bushes. It like, watches me."

"Well, just ignore it I guess, if it bothers you."

"It doesn't so much bother me but kind of creeps me out. And I don't think I can ignore it. The eyes are so, you know. They're just so..."

"Blue?" Aunt Vicki said, raising her eyebrows a tad.

"I was going to say intelligent. Like it isn't just watching me. It's observing me. Know what I mean?"

"I guess so." Aunt Vicki stared at him, unblinking.

"What?" He knew she was thinking about something when that look came over her face.

"Nothing," she said, shaking off her thoughts. She continued petting the dog. "It's been several months now, hasn't it? How's homeschooling going?"

His brow narrowed, irritated at the sudden change of subject. "You know how it's going," he muttered, not bothering to look at her. "Same old crap."

"Jay!"

"What? Same old poop then. Better?"

"Don't say that around the dogs. It gives them ideas."

Jay cracked a smile, giving Aunt Vicki what she was looking for. "There it is," she said. "I've missed that smile."

"I still smile," he insisted, now with a frown.

"Yeah, but not so much anymore. I hope home-schooling you was the right decision. Well, actually, I know it was, but I'd like to think eventually you'll agree."

"Doubtful."

Aunt Vicki sighed apologetically. "Well, we did what we had to do. The thing with the toy gun in your locker was the very last straw. You weren't meant for public school, that's all."

Jay stopped scratching the dog for a moment and turned to Aunt Vicki, a hand on each of his knees. "Not cool."

Aunt Vicki grinned with a half laugh. "What do you mean, 'not cool?'" she mocked.

"How would you feel if you were being bullied for something you didn't even do? And to top it off, then accused of doing something you didn't do by your own family? I swear, I didn't do anything. I wouldn't even know where to get a gun that looked that real."

Her smile faded. "Jay, now's not the time to—"

"And to make it even worse, instead of protecting you, your dad and aunt punished you?"

"Homeschool is not a punishment, Jay."

"Maybe not to you."

"It's not. And I believe you didn't do it. Believe it or not, I'm trying to protect you and so is your dad." Aunt Vicki blew a piece of hair away from her eye. "I mean, from Brian."

Jay huffed and scratched the dog's back, maybe a little harder than intended. When the dog flinched, he softened his touch.

Brian. He clenched his jaw at the name. Ever since Brian and Thad had taken him to his old house six months ago where Mom had died, Jay hadn't been the same. He still wondered if the lady they'd seen was Mom's ghost or her guardian angel or something, and he had nightmares about it almost every night. One thing was for certain, Brian had ruined his life in more ways than one. "I thought maybe you were protecting Brian from me. I'm the one you blamed the gun incident on."

"Oh my gosh, Jay, please. We've been over this so many times. I believe you. Brian probably did do it. All I know is that if we didn't get you out of there, you'd have been kicked out by now because of that kid. Or maybe worse."

"Seriously? You're like, so dramatic."

"Oh, no." She frowned, eyeing Jay. "Brian is bad news. I've always known that."

Jay knew it too. He cursed the day he'd decided to be his friend. If it wasn't for Brian, he'd still be in school today. He'd been a jerk since kindergarten, so how did Jay not see it coming? How did he not realize Brian would eventually turn on him too?

Brian and Thad had been his only friends before they'd grown bored of him and turned on him. Now they seemed to ferociously hate his guts. What made everything worse was that Brian was dating Lydia. Seeing them together almost crushed Jay.

Even with all of that, Jay would still go back to school if he had the chance. Just being able to see Lydia every day, even from a distance, would make it all worth it.

"Just stay away from that kid."

"Don't worry. Everyone hates me now. I can safely say I'll be staying away from everybody like you and Dad want."

Aunt Vicki sighed again. "That's not what we want. Look, I know this has been hard on you, Jay. I do. But someday you'll understand."

This brought a roll of the eyes, as he'd heard it a million times. "He stinks," Jay mumbled after a moment.

"I know. He's starting to draw flies." She grunted as she got to her feet. "Let's bathe him."

"Okay. What's his name, anyway?" Jay scratched his light brown ears, feeling the dirt going into his fingernails.

"Well, he does have a name, but I think we should give him a new one. He doesn't need any reminders of his old life."

"Hmm. Maybe I can get a new name too."

"Funny," Aunt Vicki said in a monotone, her mouth skewed to the left.

"What do you want to call him?"

"You always come up with the cool names. You'll think of something."

"How about Stinky?"

Aunt Vicki laughed. "Yes, but what'll we call him when he's clean?"

"He'll still be Stinky. He just won't stink."

She shook her head. "Right, but I'm not sure anyone will want to adopt a dog that has a reputation of smelling bad."

"Okay." When Jay stood up, the dog flinched and took a couple of tentative steps backward. "It's okay." He caressed the dog's fur until he calmed down.

"Poor little guy," Aunt Vicki said, her brow drawn tight, eyes soft with worry.

"How about Ducky?"

"Ducky?"

"Yeah, because he ducks when you try to touch him. That and it's a cool name."

"Ducky, huh? That's not too bad."

"Do you like that, Ducky?" Ducky seemed to be warming up to Jay, inching closer, looking up at him with his large, brown, doe eyes. "He wagged his tail. Did you see that? He does like it."

"You made Ducky happy, Jay. Thank you. Now let's get the stink off him."

"Okay." Jay wiped his hands on the back of his shorts. "When we're done, I'll walk Bruno."

Aunt Vicki's expression changed to one of concern, causing the smile on Jay's face to disappear.

"What? Where is he?" They'd had Bruno a very long time. He was missing part of a hind leg, which was the main reason no one had adopted him. But he was such an awesome dog, and Jay loved patiently walking him around the grounds almost every day. He was like a pseudo pet to him. It had to be that way because Dad was allergic to anything with paws.

"Aw, honey." Aunt Vicki put her hand on his shoulder gingerly, peering up into his blue eyes with her large brown ones, standing a good inch shorter than him. "Good news and bad news."

His heart ached with anticipation of what she was about to say. He sighed and swallowed hard. No way he was going to cry—at least not in here around other people.

"It's good though, Jay. It is," Aunt Vicki insisted as he pulled away from her touch.

"That's cool." His voice cracked as he tried to hold in the pain as best he could.

"They were really nice people."

"They?"

"A woman and a man. So, he'll have a momma and a dad."

Aunt Vicki was beginning to get on his nerves. If she was going to feel sorry for him, she shouldn't have allowed Bruno to be adopted in the first place. "I don't want to talk about it." Jay opened a cabinet to retrieve the dog shampoo and a towel.

She was quiet for a few seconds before relenting. "Okay. I get it. Let's bathe Ducky, then."

"Why couldn't we've just put Bruno in the backyard?" he spouted, slamming the shampoo bottle down on the counter in front of him, swallowing his emotion until his throat burst into pain and traveled up to his sinuses. "It's not fair!"

"Oh, Jay. We would if we could. Your dad—"

"I know. He's allergic. But if he's in the yard, what's the big deal?"

"It wouldn't be right to go against your dad's wishes. He can't go within two feet of them, you know that."

"What about in the guesthouse with you?"

"I already have a cat your dad's not happy with. I can't put a dog in there with her. Besides, a dog would still have to go out in the yard sometimes. You know all of this, Jay."

"It's not like Dad ever goes outside, anyway. He never leaves the freakin' house."

"Jay!" She gave him a disapproving look.

He noticed the hot girl eyeing them again and lowered his voice. "It's true." He thrust the towel into Aunt Vicki's arms. "Why did you have to give him away?" He stomped off, scaring Ducky into the corner once more. "It's not fair."

"It was the best for Bruno. We're here to rescue animals and give them good homes, not keep them in cages. Come back, Jay," Aunt Vicki called out. "We have to bathe Ducky."

Jay turned to the scared dog, then back to her. "What's the point? He's only gonna get dirty again." He sprinted out past Miss Connie, who was still at the counter, and yanked open the door.

Mis Connie croaked, "See ya', Jay," but he was too ticked off to care.

He was sick of everything—sick of being lonely, sick of not having a mom, sick of catering to his dad's insecurities, sick of Aunt Vicki and Dad not letting him have a cell phone like every other kid in the world, and he was sick of not being able to have a dog. Bruno being gone finally broke him. He couldn't fall in love with another one. At least not so soon. Besides, before long, Ducky would be gone too.

How was he going to continue on without Bruno? "This is trash!" he barked. Why did everything have to be so freaking unfair?

The gem on the ring that hung from the chain around his neck glittered red in the sunlight, catching his eye. He lifted it closer to his face. It was the only thing he had left that had belonged to his mother. Its beauty typically made him feel a little better on his most difficult days. But he was still mad. Straight-up furious.

As Jay continued to stomp down the sidewalk, fuming, he averted his gaze to see a pair of deep blue eyes observing him. It startled him at first, making him slow down his pace. Since Jay saw the strange looking dog almost daily for the last few months, he'd stopped being afraid of it. Sometimes the dog seemed to glare at him without moving or even blinking, but it never showed even a hint of hostility. It had never given him a reason to fear, yet its eyes seemed so mysterious—in a creepy sort of way.

The 35 to 40-pound dog, which appeared to be some kind of black lab mix, sat up in the grass in the same place Jay had seen it last. It moved its paws up and down as if excited to see him, panting, which made it appear to be smiling. Its teeth glowed white next to its black fur, and its tongue was very pink.

Jay frowned. Seeing the unrestrained dog made him even angrier. Its owners shouldn't allow the dog to roam the neighborhood, using everyone's lawn as its own personal toilet. Where the heck were they? Why did they choose to have a dog if they weren't going to take care of it? It could dart out into the street and get run over.

"Haven't you stupid people ever heard of a leash?" he yelled out to whoever was within hearing distance. At the sound of Jay's angry voice, the dog closed its panting mouth, turned around with its tail between its legs, and slinked off through the bushes.

Jay continued marching down the sidewalk, his vengeful attitude quenched for the moment. By the time he reached his house, guilt washed over him for scaring the black dog. The weight of scaring and abandoning Ducky hit him at the same time. He climbed the steps to the front door, dragging his feet. "I can't even get along with dogs," he whispered before retreating to his room, sulking and feeling sorry for himself.

3

CUTTING IT CLOSE

J ay tried to shove everything that happened the day before out of his mind as he ran his fingers through his short, straight, light brown hair and threw on his black Colorado Rockies cap, forming the bill. As he studied his reflection in his bedroom mirror, he thought to himself that despite being out of Lydia's league, he wasn't totally hideous. He only had a couple of zits, one dimple that showed itself sometimes when he smiled or talked, normal looking blue eyes, an average sized nose, and an okay smile.

The only thing that bugged him about his physique was his height. Because he was the youngest in his grade, he was always shorter than everyone in his old class, even Lydia. He would eventually catch up and be sixteen like everyone else, but not until August. Two long months from now. Then shortly after that everyone would begin turning seventeen, putting him behind again. Ah, the circle of life.

He stood up as straight as he could, raising his heels

off the floor. Maybe Lydia would notice him if he were taller like Brian. He made a muscle, which was more like an extension of the bone. "Humerus." He made a face as he remembered the name. Kind of an ironic word. His skinny arm was humorous compared to Brian's, that was for sure.

The door flew open, and he quickly dropped his arms, falling flat on his feet. "Hey, how's it coming?" Jay's dad, Gene, stuck his bespectacled face inside. As usual, his lenses were smudged, catching the sunlight streaming through his bedroom window. The fact that Dad never cleaned his glasses had always bugged him. Besides that, Jay was still ticked off about yesterday. When he'd come home early from the Humane Society upset about Bruno, Dad had said maybe he shouldn't go there anymore if he was going to get so attached to the animals. And really, how was that helpful?

"Can you knock?" Jay asked in a soft tone, trying to tread lightly.

"Sorry."

It wasn't like Jay hadn't asked him to many times before. He cleared his throat and turned from Dad's reflection in the mirror to the real thing. "I'm all done. Can I go now?"

"Maybe you should stay home today. Give yourself a break."

"I want to go."

"Probably not a good idea," Dad said, shaking his head. "You're emotional."

Jay slumped in exasperation. "Dude, I'm not emotional."

"Don't call me dude. Listen, if you want to go, that's fine. But I'll have to check your work first."

"Can't you check it later? I need to go." Jay timed his walk every day in the afternoon to pass Lydia's house before she got home from school. He'd never been able to speak to her like a normal person. Ever since they'd met, he'd stutter and say something he'd later regret. In fact, the last time he'd talked to her was months ago in math class when he told her, "You smell like apples." Real smooth.

"Should've thought about that yesterday before you screwed up your homework so bad. You didn't even put half an effort into those problems. You just wanted to get out of here. That's not going to fly today, my friend." Dad snatched the paperwork off the desk as Jay grunted and groaned. "Sit there until I'm done checking it."

"Come on." Jay fell into his chair, slouching and crossing his arms to his chest.

Dad plopped onto the bed in the gray sweats he wore every other day (he alternated between these and his dark blue ones with the hole in the crotch), examining each problem. Since Mom died, Dad cared nothing about his appearance. Days would go by when he didn't shave or brush his hair. In fact, if Dad was asked right at that moment when the last time he took a shower was, it would most likely take him a few minutes to recall. Yet, from the looks of the one family photo they possessed that was untouched by the fire, taken when Jay was three years old, you would get the impression that he was a very sharp man at one point.

After about five minutes of Dad thoroughly marking up two pages, he handed them back. "I see why you didn't want me to check it. Do those over. If you have questions, ask now. Otherwise, I'll be in the living room if you need me."

"Dad, can't I do it tomorrow?"

"No, you cannot."

Jay threw the papers on his desk in a fit. "You just don't want me to leave the house. Just because you never want to see the light of day doesn't mean I don't."

"Don't go there. That has nothing to do with it."

"Yes, it does! If you had your way, you wouldn't let me take a step outside, ever!"

"That's not true. I only want to protect you."

Aunt Vicki and Dad were being ridiculous. Why did they have to treat him like he was five? "Protect me from what? Why does everyone want to protect me? I don't need protection!"

"Jay, calm down."

"No, Dad. I loved Mom, too. I miss her so much and life is like hard without her. But it's been twelve years."

"Oh no, I won't listen to this." Dad pointed his finger in the air. "I won't."

"I think about her every day. Seriously, there's never a day that I don't feel like, you know, cheated because she isn't here. But I don't know, Dad. I mean, you miss her like it happened yesterday."

"Yeah, I do, Jay." Something shifted in his eyes. It was that distant, aching look Jay had seen too many times— the kind of grief that didn't shout, just lingered, heavy and quiet. And Jay hated it. For some reason, it made him feel guilty inside. "I will never stop missing her like it happened yesterday. Never. You got that? Now finish those problems, or you're going nowhere. Nothing you can say to me will change my mind."

Jay sighed. It was hard to argue with him when he had that pained look on his face. "Okay. I'll work on it."

"No questions?"

"No."

"Call me when you're done, then."

As soon as Dad disappeared, Jay grabbed the framed photo off his desk and lifted it to his face. There they were all dressed up, Mom in a dress and Dad and little Jay in suits, posing before the white trellis in the front yard of their old house.

"Mom." She was so beautiful with her long, dark hair and big, bright blue eyes. It sucked he only had the one photo of her. Many expressions and aspects of her face had disappeared from his memory forever.

Yet he still remembered some things. He recalled the feeling of her holding him close, telling him everything would be all right. Now, looking into her eyes, they seemed to say that same thing—that it would all work out. "But he's driving me crazy," Jay told her. "Why did you leave me alone with him?"

He laid the frame down and clutched the ruby ring on the chain around his neck, the same one on Mom's finger in the photo. Aunt Vicki had one just like it, only her stone was a little smaller. According to Aunt Vicki, the two sisters were given the rings by their parents when they were teenagers.

They'd found Mom's ring in the remains of the house after she died. Dad said she'd told him to give the ring to Jay if anything happened to her. She wanted him to wear it on a chain which he'd done since last year when Dad had finally decided to trust him with it.

Panic set in as he realized he had been reminiscing way too long and was running out of time. He hurried and finished his work as accurately as he could, then scrambled down the steps with the papers tight in his fist.

Dad sat in his chair with a can of soda on the table next to him. He propped his feet on the coffee table, a big toe poking out of his once white sock. The newspaper he held covered his face, his uncombed brown hair peeking over it. The headline read, *Fore! Golf Cart Thief Strikes Again—Cops 'Teed' Off.*

He took a sip of his soda just as he noticed Jay on the stairs and lowered the paper onto his lap, patting his chest, coughing. "What's up, bud?"

Jay held out his assignment and Dad inspected it with red eyes, revealing that he was either tired or had been crying. Jay thought he was most likely the cause of both.

"How'd you do?"

"It's hard."

"Everything's hard until you learn it. If it was easy, you wouldn't be learning."

Jay exhaled with exaggeration, his focus on the floor, his head cocked to the side and his shoulders slouched over.

After examining the papers, looking disappointed, Dad said, "Go get your book and we'll hash this thing out together."

"But, Dad, it's 2:30. Can we finish tomorrow?"

"You're getting this done now. How're you going to learn this stuff if we keep putting it off?"

"Fine." Jay stomped off to his room to get the book.

When he returned, Jay and Dad worked on the problems Jay didn't understand until he got them all correct. Jay sighed enough to inflate a Macy's Thanksgiving Day Parade balloon.

"Okay, looks like we got it. You're done. Good job."

His watch showed 3:16. If he booked it, he might make it past Lydia's before she got home. If he could get to the end of Mercy Lane and turn on Grant Street, she would never see him. But school had just let out, so it would be close. If Dad hadn't grounded him for a week from his bike for some stupid reason, he would've made it no problem, but now it would be tough. "I gotta bounce." He jumped out of his seat and took off for the door.

Dad uttered, "You're welcome, buddy," sarcastically under his breath right before Jay slammed the door shut.

Jay bolted down the street as if his pants were on fire, keeping his pace until he neared Lydia's house. *Maybe she isn't home yet.* His watch read 3:21. Man, he was cutting it close. He slowed down to a brisk stride, not wanting to attract too much attention while looking from her house to his shoes and back again. Lost in his own anxious thoughts, he ran smack dab into someone coming the opposite way. Books and papers flew in the air and all over the lawn. All Jay heard was, "Umph," not knowing if it had come from the person he'd run into, himself or both.

"Watch where you're going, Jay," an angry voice spouted.

Jay gasped, almost falling to his knees as his eyes focused on the beauty he had all but mowed down.

"Lydia," he whispered, too soft for human ears to hear.

4

A MEANINGFUL CONVERSATION

"Well," Lydia said, blinking at him a few times, her beautiful, shiny black hair on one shoulder and her now empty, manicured hands on her hips. "What're you waiting for? Close your mouth and help me pick all this up."

Jay found himself frozen in her presence. This was exactly what he didn't want to happen. The total opposite. He closed his gaping mouth. "S-s-sorry."

"Yeah. I'll forgive you if you help me."

"Oh, yeah. Sure." Together, they knelt down and gathered the books and papers that were strewn around the grass and on the sidewalk. A soft wind brought her scent his way, making him swoon. He was thankful he wasn't standing up for fear his legs wouldn't hold him at that moment.

"What the heck are you late for, anyway?" Lydia asked him in a manner that may have had a twinge of flirtation in it. Or maybe irritation. With Lydia, it was hard to tell.

"Nothing, I..." He stretched to retrieve a piece of

paper, freezing in place as his eyes met the dog's. It was sitting across the street with its mouth closed and its head cocked to one side, staring at him. Not at Lydia, not at both of them, but at him. A chill ran down his spine.

"Speak up, Jay." Lydia clapped her hands once, grabbing back his attention.

"Just on my way to, um, work."

"You work?" She sounded mildly impressed as they both got to their feet.

"Kind of. I help at the Humane Society. I don't get paid."

"It's not work if you don't get paid, is it?" She scanned the area to make sure they'd recovered all her belongings.

"I'm gonna be a veterinarian, so it helps me get experience."

"That's cool. What else you been up to? Still getting *home-schooled*?" She used the word in a tone that made it sound beneath her.

"Yeah." Jay could feel his palms getting slick and his heart palpitating. He didn't want to have this conversation with Lydia and risk saying something stupid. He didn't want to talk about what was sure to come up, and he didn't want to run into the person he desperately wanted to avoid, even more than Lydia, although not for the same reasons.

"Do you like it?"

Jay glimpsed behind her, at her house, up the street, then back to her again as he spoke. "Like what?" he asked absently.

She leaned in, raising her voice as if speaking to the deaf. "Being *home-schooled*."

"Oh. It's okay."

"Brian isn't here. You don't have to worry."

"I'm not." Jay touched the bill of his cap and pushed it further down in the back, not knowing what to do with his fidgeting hands. He desperately needed to get out of there but wanted to do so without coming off rude or wimpy.

"Really?" She squinted at him.

"No."

"Hmm. Well, you should be. You really screwed him over. I know all about it." Her hand flew back to one hip, her books balanced on the other.

"I didn't screw him over."

"Yes, you did. You totally did. You said you knew nothing about that stupid toy gun in you guys' gym locker, he got suspended, and we both know you knew all about it."

"I wasn't lying." A bead of sweat dripped down Jay's temple. He knew she didn't believe him any more than she would believe a habitual liar, which she and the others apparently thought he was considering they'd called him one enough times.

"You gonna admit it or what?"

"I don't know what you mean." Jay heard a faint growl and peered around Lydia to find the dog baring its teeth.

Lydia turned to see what Jay was looking at. As she did, the dog legit ducked back behind the bushes, but not before it was spotted. "What's up with your dog?"

"That's not my dog. It just watches me all the time."

Lydia's glare let him know he'd just said the stupidest thing she'd ever heard. Worse than the apple remark. "Whatever. No one's here. Stop denying what happened and tell the truth for once." Her expression transformed as she batted her thick, beautiful eyelashes, gazing at him with her big brown eyes. He felt like he was melting in them. "Come on, Jay. You can tell me." Her tone was now sticky sweet.

"I don't know how it got there," he explained, hypnotized by her eyes. Her olive-colored skin on her gorgeous Latino face glimmered in the bright Colorado sun. "I've told you."

At his response, her voice switched back to its original annoyance. "Come on. You set him up. He ticked you off when he got you in trouble after you two cheated on that math quiz, and you got your revenge."

Her attitude snapped him out of his trance, her emotions playing ping pong with his brain. "I never cheated. Brian set me up."

"Please. How can you be so innocent?"

"I'm not innocent. But I'm also not a liar."

"If what you're saying is true," Lydia said with a shake of her head, "what reason would he have to set you up?"

Jay had his suspicions. Almost certainly it was because he knew Jay had feelings for Lydia. More than a few times, Brian had caught Jay boring a hole into the back of her sweet-smelling head during math class. "All I know is after he got caught, he told Mr. Merritt I let him cheat, but I didn't know anything about it. Then this gun shows up. I have no idea how he did it, but it was all him."

"Come on. That's not the story I heard."

"Well, that's the truth," he replied with sudden bravery.

"How come you never told me about this before?"

"Please. It's not like we've sat down and had meaningful conversations."

Lydia raised her thick, manicured eyebrows. "Meaningful conversation? Is that what you want?"

Unsure how to respond, he opened his mouth, but nothing came out.

"Let's go have a meaningful conversation." She extended her graceful, long-fingered hand for him to take while struggling with her books on her other arm. "'K?" She smiled at him sweetly, and he could almost see the devil in it.

Jay took her hand with apprehension, not sure what else to do, knowing he couldn't deny her. Together, they walked to Lydia's house as his brain went haywire. *I can't believe this is happening. Where're we going? I hope my palms aren't sweaty and gross. I wonder if she's still with Brian.*

"Don't you think it would be nice if you carried my books?" Lydia asked, interrupting his thoughts.

"What?"

"They're hurting my arm."

"Oh, sorry." He took the books from her, wondering briefly why the girl didn't carry a backpack. He had to remove his hand from hers for just a second, then softly replaced it. A chill went through him at her touch.

"Thanks."

Jay avoided eye contact, knowing if he looked into her mesmerizing eyes once more, he would probably freak out and drop her books all over the ground again. That is a humiliation that would surely cause his death.

He followed Lydia's lead as she took him through her front yard to the gate. She opened the latch, and they entered the backyard. He watched her hair bounce as she walked in front of him. He'd memorized her head from math class, and the familiarity of it felt comforting in a strange way.

Jay had loved her as soon as she'd strolled into the classroom for the first time in the beginning of ninth grade last year after she moved there from California. Even when she started dating Brian in the middle of the year, he still hadn't been able to keep his eyes off her. His soul had been crushed, but his love never faded. He hadn't had the guts to talk to her then. All he could do was stare at the back of her gorgeous head and smell her.

But that seemed like ages ago, and now here he was holding her cold hand as they walked together. It was like a dream. He wondered if she noticed how nervous he was and that his heart was pounding out of control in his chest.

She collected her books from him and set them down on the grass as they settled underneath a window in the backyard. "So, what do you want to talk about?" she asked him, leaning up against the house, her long hair on her left shoulder and her head cocked questionably.

Jay had no idea what to say to her. He'd imagined many times being near her, holding her, kissing her, laughing at something—at what? None of his daydreams ever consisted of conversation. How could he have let himself be so unprepared?

"Or was this your plan to get me alone?"

"P-plan?"

Lydia inched closer to him. He felt her warm breath on his face. It smelled vaguely of cinnamon. She touched his now-short hair, shooting a sharp shiver down his spine. "I liked your hair long. When exactly did you decide to give it all up and become a brainiac?"

"I-I'm not..."

"You've always wanted to kiss me, haven't you, Jay?" The way she said his name started his heart to pump even faster, which seemed impossible only moments before. "Close your mouth and make your move," she breathed, her full, red lips making every word sound as if it dripped with honey. "Unless you're thinking of Frenching me."

Jay shut his mouth, unaware that it had been gaping open again. French kissing was not something he wanted to attempt with Lydia. At least not yet. A hundred percent, he'd mess it up. Then she'd definitely think he was a geek. But he had to do something. He couldn't just not kiss her.

He moved in closer, not believing what was happening. It was too good to be true. As he puckered his wet lips and closed his eyes in anticipation, a sharp tap on the shoulder made him aware of a presence behind him. His eyes popped open, his lips still ready for action. Lydia was not in front of him anymore. He seemed to be about to make out with an invisible girl.

His first thought was that her parents had caught them, but the truth was even worse. He turned his head to find Brian, Thad, and another guy he knew from school named Smith, all three with their thick arms crossed in front of them.

"Crap," he uttered through his still tightly puckered lips.

5

HE WHO FLEES AND RUNS AWAY…

Brian yanked Jay up by the collar, knocking him off balance and shaking every good feeling Jay ever had right out of him, as if what had just happened, or almost happened, had never occurred.

Brian was only about six months older than Jay, but he'd always had more muscle than Jay's thin frame. Even if Jay worked out with weights every day, he wouldn't obtain even a fraction of the muscle Brian had just by existing. He was also a lot tanner than Jay. Then again, 99.9 percent of the population was darker than Jay's pasty skin.

"That's all you gotta say, clown?" Brian yelled, sounding like a movie villain knockoff, strands of black hair hanging over his angry hazel eyes. He always did this fake New York gangster voice when he wanted to sound tough, which just made him sound even more like an idiot.

"Nothing happened," Jay squeaked. Brian yanked Jay's collar tighter, cutting off his air, and leaned in close, his breath hot on Jay's face. Smith, who was seventeen and should have been a senior but failed a grade when he was in middle school, and Thad, sixteen, stood behind Brian looking like a couple of big, dumb apes.

"What, Gay? I can't hear a word you're saying. You sound like a whimpering cat!" Snickers from the groupies followed. Jay had no idea if Lydia was one of them or not. He wondered to himself what the heck a 'whimpering cat' might sound like. This dude truly had no brain.

Jay coughed and raised his voice. "I said nothing happened, Brian."

Brian let him go and Jay's feet planted back on the grass as he steadied himself. "You're really gonna stand there and lie like that?"

"Seriously," Jay reinstated firmly, rubbing his neck to get the blood moving again.

"I freakin' saw you, bro! I seen you stickin' your face up to my girl and whatever. You kissed her, didn't you?"

"No."

"You always liked her!"

Jay's gaze traveled to where Lydia stood, her back up against the house, examining her nails. She glanced up and shook her head at him. As they stared into each other's eyes, he couldn't help but wonder, had she set him up for this?

"Don't look at her, you freak!" Brian pushed him down with both hands to his shoulders. Jay landed on his butt in the grass, hard enough to knock the wind out of him along with every bit of his dignity. He heard laughter again over his heavy breathing and pounding heart.

Jay squinted in the sun to find Smith, with strawberry blond hair, fair freckled skin, and a fat nose that lay flat on his face like someone had punched it a few times into its shape, approach him. His heavy set frame blocked the sun like a solar eclipse as he effortlessly pulled Jay up by his collar, which at this point was probably stretched beyond repair, until he was all the way back up on his feet.

Smith threw his fat fist back to punch him but stopped when Jay yelled, "You have to have these guys beat me up, Brian?" He tightened his face to prepare for impact. "Can't do it yourself?"

"Wait," Brian ordered. "He's right." He cracked his knuckles as he made his way toward Jay like a cliché right out of a bad movie. "Let him go. I wanna do it myself." He laughed.

Smith dropped him and stepped back. A white roll of belly fat hung in the gap between the bottom of his shirt and the waist of his jeans. He kept his enormous, pink fists clenched and ready, just in case.

Jay didn't know what to do, so he just stared at Brian in anticipation. His bottom lip quivered out of nervousness completely beyond his control. He clamped his mouth tight to still it.

"You screwed me once and everything and I guess you decided to screw me again," Brian said through gritted teeth.

"I never screwed anyone." Smith and Thad snickered again, and it took half a second for Jay to catch onto it.

Brian scowled. "What makes you think you can show up around here and everything after what you did?" He had a habit of overusing the words whatever and everything. At that moment, if Jay heard either word one more time, he thought he might lose it. "You let me take the rap and whatever and you run off and dip outta school? You jerk! You know I was like grounded forever 'cause of that."

"You expected me to take the blame?"

"I expected you to man up." Brian scanned him up and down in disgust, then stepped toward him, his face so close Jay could smell what he thought might be the residual of Cheetos. "It wasn't mine, and you know it!"

"Right," Thad said dumbly. Thad was Brian's first cousin and was at least a foot taller than all of them. He had short, stubby, dark hair, broad shoulders, and a face full of zits.

"Well, it wasn't mine," Jay said.

"Liar!" Brian yelled so loud that an uncontrolled chunk of spit flew out of his mouth and whizzed past Jay's head, barely missing him. "But you didn't get punished at all. You left me there to take all the blame at school and everything. I got suspended for a couple weeks and grounded and yelled at every day for a damn month. What did you get? You stay home and play video games all day and whatever and get home-schooled by your crazy daddy." He turned behind him to Thad and Smith, then chuckled as they appeared to share an inside joke. "Then again, maybe you're the one worse off." He received more laughter from this, as expected, turning his attention back to Jay. "Your dad went straight-up crazy after your mom got all burned up and whatever."

Jay's fists clenched, and his jaw tightened.

"The only thing that psycho is teaching you is to hide from the world and whatever, just like he does. Has he even seen the light of day since your momma died?"

"Leave my parents out of this."

"Fine. I'll just destroy you and get it over with. How's

that?" Before he could prepare himself, Brian's fist came out of nowhere and hit Jay's right eye, making it feel like it would pop inside his head. The force of it caused his cap to fly off and land somewhere next to him, followed by whooping from Smith and Thad. It took him a while to refocus his eyes back on the angry Brian, who wasn't finished.

"You seriously come here and make moves on my girl? After all you've done to me already?" He hauled off and punched Jay again, this one landing on his jaw.

Jay tasted blood as he flew back to the ground, throwing his arms in front of him to block any additional punches. The right side of his face ached and throbbed. Blurry versions of the trio of idiots loomed over him as they cheered and hooted.

Out of the midst of it, he heard Lydia scream for Brian to stop. "You're gonna get in trouble again! He's learned his lesson, okay?" Lydia pulled Brian away from Jay for a moment before he shrugged her off.

"No, Lydia. I don't think he's learned anything. Get out of my way!"

"Go, Jay!" Lydia waved her hands, shooing him off. "What're you waiting for?"

Realizing this was the break he needed, Jay gathered himself, scrambled to his feet and took off running down the street toward the Humane Society, struggling to keep his balance.

Jay was into streaming nature docs on Netflix and YouTube. He remembered watching one about lions hunting their prey. In it, they quoted a saying: *He who flees and runs away, lives to fight another day*. That seemed to fit his current situation appropriately. He felt just like a zebra running from a pride of lions. Mentally challenged lions anyway.

The sound of footsteps behind him cut through the pounding in his ears, fading as he ran. They must have known it was no use to try to catch him. He could outrun anyone at school and had won several first-place ribbons in track to prove it. Even with a throbbing head that felt like a ripe melon on his shoulders, and even though he was having trouble focusing his eyes and his legs seemed to be made of rubber, he was fast. Later, he would be angry at himself for running away like that, like a scared little girl. But for now, all he thought about was removing himself as far away and as quickly as possible.

Through the ringing vibrating in his brain, he faintly heard Smith and Thad yelling obscenities after him, along with Lydia and Brian arguing.

Above it all, somewhere close by, a dog howled.

6

A WORD OF THANKS

"Dad will never let me hear the end of this," Jay told his reflection in the bathroom mirror the next morning. A shiner about the size and shade of a plum puffed up around his right eye. His jaw throbbed, his lip was fat and split, and his head pounded with the worst headache of his life.

Aunt Vicki was understandably upset when she laid eyes on him after his beatdown. She had him stay at the Humane Society until closing, then they went to McDonalds afterward. Once home, she shooed him up to his room so she could talk to Dad before he saw him. Dad freaked out about pretty much anything and everything since the fire, but Aunt Vicki could keep him calm in almost any situation.

Dad expected him downstairs at any minute. A nervous twinge twisted in his stomach at the thought of his reaction. "I need an aspirin." He found an Advil in the cabinet and swallowed it down with water from the tap before tiptoeing down the steps to the living room. "This sucks," he mumbled to himself, raking a hand through his hair, remembering that he'd lost his favorite ball cap in the ambush. While descending the staircase, he scanned the area. Dad was nowhere.

Every morning, Dad put his schoolwork assignments on the dining room table for Jay to complete while he traded stocks in his office, which he had done ritually since Mom died. But the tabletop was empty outside of a cereal bowl half full of milk with three or four O's floating in it and an empty glass with orange residue identifying what it had once contained. "Really, take all the time you want," he whispered. "Please."

He opened the screen door to grab the paper for Dad, as he did most mornings. Something was blocking his path on the concrete before him. Happiness flooded him when he realized what it was. "My Rockies cap." It was damp and stretched out like someone had been playing tug of war with it, but at least he had it back. But how? Who would have put it there? "Lydia."

Lydia must have come by yesterday after the confrontation, maybe too nervous to ring the bell. Perhaps too shy? No. Not Lydia. But she *did* bring it to him. That's all that mattered. But why would she take the time to do that and also risk Brian finding out? There could only be one reason. She had exposed her secret, possibly unknowingly. "She likes me." Was it true? Jay's legs turned to jelly as he held his cap close to his chest, sighing like a lovesick puppy.

"Hey," a voice boomed behind him.

His body and heart jumped simultaneously, causing him to drop the cap. "Dang it! You scared me," he told his dad in an irritated, brave voice. Remembering his eye, he shifted to an angle where it would be less noticeable.

"Oh Lord," Dad said in a whiney voice that annoyed him like fingernails on a chalkboard. "Vicki told me about your fight. Let me see it." He put his hand on Jay's swollen jaw, turning it toward him to get a better view through the smudges in his old, worn-out glasses. "She said it wasn't that bad. This is horrendous."

"It wasn't *my* fight."

"Well, whose fight was it? Don't tell me you were an innocent bystander." Dad grimaced and made a hissing sound through his teeth. Jay dodged his touch, backing away.

"They jumped me, Dad."

"Vicki told me. I don't understand. Why would they do that?"

"I don't know."

"You don't know? How do you not know?"

Jay shrugged. He almost threw his cap on before noting it had some unidentified, slimy substance on it, then slammed the door.

"You mean to say you were walking along, minding your own business, and these boys just jumped on you and started punching you?"

"Pretty much."

"Not sure I buy that, Son." Dad shook his head in exasperation, pushing his glasses higher on his nose. "I just don't get why you won't talk to me about this. Tell me what happened and let me help you."

"Look, I told you. It's the same as always. They're pissed because they think I set him up."

"Brian?"

"Yeah. They think that fake gun was mine, and I let him take the fall and that's why you pulled me out of school so no one would find out. You know all about this, Dad. Nothing's changed." Jay slinked over to the couch and landed on it with a plop, already over it.

"I still don't get where this gun came from."

"Dad, we've been over this so many freakin' times." Jay rolled his eyes up to the ceiling, worn out from previous conversations. "I don't know."

"You never seem to know anything."

Jay gritted his teeth and closed his eyes. Dad would never believe him no matter what he said, so why try?

"You need some ice on that eye. You should've done that last night."

"I'm fine."

"This is exactly why you just need to stay home."

"I'm not hibernating forever. No way. I told you, I'm fine."

Dad sighed. "Let's just get to work."

"I don't feel like doing schoolwork. Can't we take a day off?"

"You certainly can't. You can't blow everything off when things don't go your way."

Jay mumbled under his breath, "Why not? You do."

"What did you say?"

"Nothing," he moaned. "I'm coming."

JAY ENDED UP GETTING GROUNDED FOR TWO DAYS FOR getting his face pounded, which was so very wrong. He recognized the real problem: It would take Dad a while to get over Jay's busted up face and feel okay about him leaving the house again. But he couldn't keep him locked up forever, although it was obvious he wanted to.

The worst part of this whole thing was that he couldn't go to the Humane Society and "accidentally" run into Lydia again. He finally wanted to talk to her. To thank her for returning his cap. And now he couldn't. Life was so ironic and unfair.

"I guess it doesn't have to be," he told himself.

When it was dark, around 9:30, Jay tiptoed down the stairs to the back door. Dad always got up early and went to bed early. Once he fell asleep, he was like a rock. Still, Jay made sure to be extra quiet. The flicker of blue light from the guesthouse window was a sure sign Aunt Vicki was stretched out on the couch, watching TV.

He wasn't sure what he would do when he got to Lydia's house. Maybe he wouldn't do anything at all. All he knew was he had a strong desire to see her—or, if nothing else, merely imagine her there behind the walls and telepathically tell her how much he appreciated the gesture.

Moving carefully, he rolled his bike out through the creaky side gate, the cool air brushing his face as he circled around to the front of the house, trying not to make a sound. Dad had grounded him from riding his bike, but since he was already breaking the rules, what did it matter? He took a left on the road out of his cul-de-sac onto Mercy Lane in the bright, full moonlight, pumping the pedals as hard as his legs would go up the hill.

Soon, Lydia's house came into view, and he braked in front of the empty driveway. All the windows were lit up except one. He was pretty sure which room was hers. It had to be the one with the purple ruffled curtains on the second floor. He focused on it, wondering if she was inside—maybe doing her homework, reading a book, or on the phone with Brian. His smile faded with that thought. As he maneuvered his bike around to leave, he snuck another peek over his shoulder at the window he imagined was hers. "Thanks, Lydia. Someday, I will thank you in person with a kiss," he said softly.

A rustle, followed by a sound that could've been a snort, came from the bushes to his right. His head whipped around, eyes narrowing. A crash within the house caused him to turn back again and nearly fall off the bike. A deep male voice followed, along with an angry yell of correction and some horrible choking coughs. Then Lydia's voice, "Whatever, Frank. Leave me alone!" This was accompanied by another crash, deep and jarring, like wood splintering. Maybe a door being kicked in.

Months ago, when they were friends, Brian had told him that Lydia lived with her mom and her mom's husband. Lydia, he'd said, couldn't stand him and didn't consider him to be her stepdad. She was a daddy's girl, but her Daddy was some bigwig who worked at the Department of Defense in D.C. and was way too busy with his life there to visit her much.

The front screen door flew open with a bang, and before Jay could duck out unseen, Lydia appeared, making him freeze in his tracks and forget all about the weird noise from the bushes.

"Who's there?" Lydia asked, unmoving, seeming frightened at the sight of his shadowy figure. "Brian?"

"No." Jay's voice cracked. He cleared his throat. "It's, it's Jay."

"What the heck are you doing here?" She stepped down off the porch and approached him, looking like the silhouette of an angel with the light glowing behind her. His heart beat in sync with her every step.

"Nothing. I happened to be in the area, that's all."

"Jay, it's like ten o'clock. Why are you 'in the area'?" She made air quotes as she grew closer. His cheeks turned hot, but she didn't seem to notice it in the dark. "Well?" she asked again, stopping a few feet from him with her arms crossed and her dark hair catching the glow of the streetlamp, shimmering with a hint of blue. "You stalking me?"

"No. What?"

"You into getting beat up or something?"

His brow narrowed, unsure how to respond.

"Hello?"

He had forgotten the words he'd planned to speak, although he had practiced several times in the mirror in case he ran into her again.

"Why are you looking at me like that?" she asked, squinting at him through the darkness.

Jay closed his gaping mouth. She never ceased to make it fall open. He was sure he looked like a total dufus to her. "Like what?"

"You're like gawking or whatever. Why are you doing that? Why are you here, Jay?"

The words slowly returned to his brain as he tried to gain the courage to speak. When he opened his mouth to do so, she interrupted him with a soft gasp, getting so close that he could make out every facial feature.

"What the heck!" She put her hand up to Jay's right eye. "He really got you good, didn't he?" She gasped again. "Whoa, your jaw looks swollen too. And your lip's busted." With the tips of her fingers, she gently touched it, and he backed away. "Sorry." She made a noise with her teeth. "I bet it hurts."

"Naw." He covered his swollen eye. It did hurt. It hurt like heck, like a million pinpricks to the face, but he wasn't about to tell her that. "Not a big deal."

"It is a big deal. I'm sorry he laid into you, Jay. I never wanted that to happen. It's probably best you stay away from me, really. I mean, it's only gonna happen again if you don't." Lydia's eyes showed concern. In his heart, Jay knew she truly cared about him. "What, Jay? You're doing it again."

"Sorry." He turned away.

"You heard all that," she said with embarrassment, pointing her thumb behind her. "Didn't you?"

"Yeah." Jay's heart went out to her. He tried not to let it show, although it was difficult.

"It's nothing." She re-crossed her arms and lifted her chin smugly. Jay saw right through it. He understood. Many times, he'd also camouflaged himself as a strong person so people wouldn't feel sorry for him because of his mom. It sucks when people feel sorry for you.

Jay nodded, not sure what to say. "Sure. I mean, parents fight." As soon as the words left his mouth, he knew he had chosen incorrectly and wished he could grab them out of the air and stuff them into his pockets before they disappeared into her ears.

Her beautiful face contorted into an ugly one before him as she huffed. "Frank is not my dad."

"Well, I mean—"

"Frank can never measure up to my dad."

"I'm sorry. I didn't mean to say that."

"It's fine. Like I said, it's nothing. I just have to put up with that moron for a few more years before I'm out of here."

"Where are you going?" Jay asked as if she were leaving tomorrow.

She shrugged. "Maybe D.C. I could join the military like my dad."

There was a base thirty-minutes away in the town over. He wanted to tell her they could run away, and he'd join the military with her. Maybe that would make him sound a little desperate. "Sounds like a good idea," he said instead.

She studied Jay's wounds as he readjusted himself on his bike. "Yikes. That looks rough. You can't even see your dimple anymore." She touched his swollen jaw. "I like that dimple."

A smile attempted to take over Jay's face and he held it back as best he could. Before he could respond, the screen door banged open once more and Lydia's hand snapped like a magnet to her side. "Lydia, you out here? Ma's looking for you. Who you talking to?" It was Scott, Lydia's older brother. He was a senior and friends with Brian. Scott only meant trouble.

"No one. Just a friend."

"What are you doing here, Jay? Didn't you get your beating yesterday?"

"Shut up, Scott," Lydia barked over her shoulder.

"Jay, what *are* you doing here, anyway?" Lydia asked,

loud enough for Scott to hear and take the hint that she didn't know either.

"Um, nothing. Just wanted to say thanks."

"For what?" Lydia asked with a confused expression that appeared genuine. Then she whispered, "For your own good, just go."

"For my cap. Thanks for that," he whispered back.

She crinkled her nose and sighed. "Whatever. You're so weird sometimes. Go home." She spun around and headed toward her house.

"Lydia," Jay said as quiet as possible to keep Scott from overhearing. He needed to ask something he'd been thinking about since the day before. He had to know.

She turned to face him. "Yeah?"

"Did you know that was gonna happen? I mean yesterday with Brian? Was it a setup?"

Her face showed no emotion. "No," she answered, and whipped her head around and walked back, wiggling her hips in her jean shorts. Jay watched her for a moment before pedaling away.

After the door banged shut, he turned for one last glimpse. Scott was still outside in the porch light, scrutinizing him with his arms crossed.

Jay grinned. He couldn't care less about Scott or even Brian, for that matter. He had what he'd come for. It was all he needed to know.

7

SAVING JAY

J ay stared at the big, cloudless Colorado sky, taking in a long, deep breath through his nose as he strolled down the street at a brisk pace. "Thank you," he whispered to no one in particular, so happy to be out of the house at least for the afternoon.

He'd gotten the impression Aunt Vicki had something to do with his freedom. Around lunchtime, less than five minutes after Dad had gotten off the phone with her, he reluctantly told Jay he could go to the Humane Society, sending Jay from frustration to jubilation with those few words. "Today's gonna be a great day!" He had a good feeling about it.

His heartbeat amplified only a bit this time compared to usual as he approached Lydia's house. No sign of life reflected in or around it. It was only two o'clock, way too early for her to be home. He slowed down as he passed, inspecting the ruffled curtains of her theoretical window, mulling their conversation from the night before over in his brain. He hadn't been able to stop thinking about it.

His stomach flipped as he remembered how concerned she'd been. He touched his jaw just as she had, realizing he now barely felt the pain. "This day just keeps getting better."

A loud rustling made him jump and he twisted around to face whoever was following him, prepared for the worst. But nothing was there. His heart beat faster and he had to remind himself to breathe as he tried to calm down, shaking his head, angry with himself for being such a wimp.

He picked up his pace. Seconds later, he heard it again. *Maybe the wind.* He slowed, listening carefully, his fear now overrun by curiosity as he was bound and determined to get behind this mystery that suddenly plagued him.

Before giving the source of the noise a chance to make it again, he whipped his head around in mid-step to catch the familiar black dog's head ducking behind a bush. His body relaxed, deflating the air that he'd been holding in his lungs, and laughed. "You've got to be kidding me. You're following me now?" he asked the dog in disbelief. "Am I being stalked by a dog?" He shook his head before muttering, "Not only that, but I'm talking to it and asking it questions! I'm losing it."

He approached the bush and reached out his hand as the dog shrunk deeper into it. "Come here. I'm not gonna hurt you. You must know that, or you wouldn't be following me." The animal's shiny blue eyes seemed to radiate a strange understanding through the leaves. Tentatively it stepped out, revealing only it's head. This time the dog remained steady as Jay's hand went under its nose. It didn't smell his hand, which seemed odd.

Instead, turned away, appearing annoyed. It did, however, allow Jay to pet its soft fur. But when he reached for its tag, the dog jerked away and barked twice in warning, making Jay jump back. "Not cool, dog!" he scolded. "You scared the crap out of me."

Jay turned to go, deciding it wasn't worth the risk of getting bit. With his first step, he ran right into a person standing in front of him and he gasped in alarm. The impact didn't seem to faze Jay's obstruction at all, as if he'd collided with a statue constructed in the middle of the sidewalk.

But it wasn't a statue. It was Brian, and he looked ticked.

"Hey, Gay," he said manically, his arms folded and his nose in the air. Jay could see right up it and wished he had a tissue to offer him. Totally gross.

"Hey, Brian," Jay replied, deepening his voice in an attempt to sound cool, but unable to mask the quiver in it.

"Heard you was hanging outside my girlfriend's house last night. Looking in her windows?" His dark hair hung in his face, and he jerked his head to shake it off.

Jay scrunched his nose, his brow narrowing. "No." He thought of Scott and didn't have to wonder how Brian knew about his nighttime rendezvous with Lydia.

Brian's right hand emerged from his crossed arms and pushed Jay backward with two fingers to his shoulder blade. "That's not what I heard."

Not again. A low rumble made him dart his eyes to the side only for a second, afraid to take his eyes off Brian for too long. Behind Brian, Jay found the dog crouching on the lawn baring its teeth.

"Would you like another black eye and whatever to match the one I gave you yesterday?" Brian shoved him again, harder this time, which about made him lose his footing. "Well? I asked you a question, Gay." He pushed him once more. Jay's shoulder shot up sparks of pain. "I got all day. I skipped school just so we could hang out and everything. Been sitting here waiting for you." Again, he poked the same shoulder. "You wanna hang, Gay?"

The dog's growl grew more prominent until Brian began to take notice. "And your stupid dog's been here with me. Sitting there watching me and whatever with its stupid, creepy, blue eyes. Dumb thing barely blinks."

"It does like to stare," Jay told him, unable to blink himself.

This set something off in Brian. He gritted his teeth and pounced on Jay like a lion, grabbing his shirt and getting right up into his face. "Don't talk to me like you're my friend. You ain't my friend!"

"What do you want, Brian?" Jay asked with the smallest twinge of bravery. Brian yanked him into Lydia's yard by the front of his shirt, moving fast enough to cause Jay to stumble over his own feet. "Whoa!" he yelped, hearing the fabric rip. By some miracle, he remained upright as he attempted to keep up with Brian's pace. "Hold up, dude."

Behind some bushes in front Lydia's wooden fence, Brian let go, his face inches from his, his bushy black eyebrows narrowing into an intense frown. "You wanna know what I want?" It was like he was reliving yesterday, this time in a parallel universe where everything was opposite. He had run into Brian just like he had Lydia, and as happy as Jay was with her yesterday, close to where he was standing with Brian now, he was scared to death in equal measure. "Well, do ya'?"

"Sure," Jay answered unenthusiastically, running his palms over his now stretched out t-shirt in a vain attempt to salvage it.

"I want you to confess and whatever."

Jay said nothing, his brow narrowing.

"I want you," Brian poked Jay in the chest with his forefinger with every other word he spit out, "to tell Principal Bowmen the truth."

Jay backed up to put some space between them. "I did tell her the truth."

Brian's face grew beet red. It seemed he could explode at any moment, which got Jay to thinking maybe he should just agree to whatever he wanted him to do, no matter if he intended on doing it or not. But his pride wasn't allowing it. "I mean the *real* truth," Brian said through gritted teeth. "It was your gun or whatever. You tell her that and you tell my dad that, and I'll never bother you again or nothin'."

"I'm not lying so you won't kill me, Brian." He had no idea where the gun had come from and wasn't about to take the rap for it, no matter how many times he got beaten.

Brian grabbed Jay by his shirt again. "That's it, Gay! I don't get why you're doing this and whatever, but this is done. If I have to break your jaw, it's gonna stop! You already got me into so much trouble at home and everything, it really don't matter anymore. I'll kill you if I have to!"

Jay gulped at the word "break" and squinted at "kill," his stomach tightening. He clenched his jaw to prepare for the impact. Brian was angry enough to not only break his jaw, but he would most certainly shatter it.

"You trying to kiss my girl is the last straw."

"I didn't do anything," Jay choked out. "She likes *me*."

Brian threw his head back and let loose a bellowing laugh, lurching Jay's head up painfully as he tightened the grip on his shirt. "That's a good one, loser! You should be a comedian."

Jay frowned, trying to squirm free and grasping Brian's hands to pry them away, but it did absolutely no good. "Let go."

"She likes you, huh? If she loves you so much, why did she trick you?"

"She didn't." Jay stopped squirming to glare at him.

"Yeah, she did, dummy. Why do you think I showed up right when I did, stupid?" Spit flew from Brian's mouth and into Jay's face with every insult.

Crap. He was actually making perfect sense. She'd totally made a fool of him. He really was an idiot.

Brian couldn't stop laughing at his humiliation. "She totally played you, moron!"

Jay was starting to think maybe he did deserve to get beaten up. He actually did try to take Brian's girl and made an utter fool of himself in the process. What did it matter anymore? "Fine. You're right. I give up. Hit me already, you jerk."

Brian drew his fist back as far as it would go as Jay closed his eyes tight in preparation for impact. The next thing he knew, Jay was flat on his back with Brian above him, screeching like a woman in a horror movie. When Jay refocused and his brain caught up with the current situation, he found the black dog had attached itself to Brian's back, its teeth sunk into his shoulder.

"Whoa!" Jay thought about running away again, but once was humiliating enough. Instead, he decided to hang around to see what would happen. He backed up a bit, maneuvering his legs under him and pulling himself to his feet. This was sure to be an interesting show.

The sound of Brian's wailing was ear-splitting as he struggled to swat at the dog clinging to his back. The poor animal's legs flailed helplessly like a rag doll, tossed around by Brian's frantic movements. "Get this thing off me!" Brian howled between high-pitched screams of agony. "Get it off! Get it off!"

Yeah, right, so you can get back to wrecking me? Jay watched Brian flail, screaming like a little girl with a spider on her back. Brian backed up and smacked the dog against the house as it yelped in pain and fell to the ground like a wet bag of sand, still and silent. Jay gasped as Brian grimaced, holding his shoulder that was rapidly soaking his shirt with blood. He kicked the dog hard with his sneaker and it flew into the air with a pitiful cry, landing on its other side. "Stupid freakin' dog!" Brian growled between clenched teeth.

The dog whined softly. Jay was more concerned for it than for Brian yet he resisted his instinct to run to its side for a moment. He needed to distract Brian so he wouldn't kick it again. "Man, you need to have that bite looked at. What if it has rabies?"

"Rabies? Aw, you gotta be freakin' kidding me!" Brian's face grew red as he scrunched it up tight, turning while reaching for his back unsuccessfully, reminding Jay of a dog chasing its tail.

"Naw, definitely. I work at the Humane Society, and I know. Dogs will attack if they have rabies."

"You sicked that dog on me, Gay!" Brian was on the verge of tears, seeming to hold them back with all his might.

"No. For real, I didn't. It's not even my dog. I—"

"Shut up! I know you did. This ain't over. Not by a long shot." He staggered off. "You suck!"

Brian bolted for the next-door neighbor's house. The lady that answered seemed to recognize him, and she rushed him inside, hysterical at the sight.

Jay fell on his knees beside the dog as it peered up at him with a strange expression of sadness and pain. Small clumps of its black hair floated in the air around its body like dark fairies.

"Thank you," Jay said, not feeling silly at all as he talked to it, unlike he had moments before. "I don't know why you did that. But thank you." The dog uttered a weak whine in response. "I'm gonna get you some help, don't you worry." With a little effort, and as gently as he could, he lifted the forty-pound dog as if it weighed nothing and ran down the sidewalk as swift as a gazelle, all the way to the Humane Society.

8

3535 MERCY LANE

Aunt Vicki gasped as Jay burst through the door of the backroom with a bang, panting and covered in sweat. "What on earth?" She dropped everything and ran to him, the dog still unmoving in his arms. He hadn't stopped to check if it was unconscious or dead. The poor thing hadn't moved the whole way.

"What happened to her?" she asked, wide-eyed and frantic.

How does she know the dog is a her? He himself didn't know if it was a boy or a girl, and he saw it almost every day. However, the thought disappeared as quickly as it had come.

"Some jerk," he told her through rapid breaths, "smacked her up against a wall and kicked her."

"What?" Aunt Vicki's mouth flew open in alarm, unable to take her fearful eyes off the unmoving dog.

"Can you help me?" he grunted. "She's heavy."

"Lay her here! Lay her here, Jay! Hurry!" She

motioned to a metal table in the middle of the room. "You really shouldn't have moved her."

Jay obeyed as she inspected the poor dog. "I couldn't just leave her there. She saved me from a severe beating."

Aunt Vicki's head shot up as her eyes met Jay's, concern and confusion on her face. "Again?" Without waiting for a response, her attention went back to her patient. "We need to elevate her head." She handed Jay a blanket and with care, lifted the dog's head as he balled it up and tucked it underneath. Jay noticed a bit of blood on one of its nostrils and a scab from an older injury on the bridge of its nose. Its eyes fluttered open halfway, and they locked onto Jay's, appearing frightened, concerned, something.

"Is she gonna be okay?" he asked.

"I sure hope so. Her eyes are open, at least. That's a good sign." Aunt Vicki gently felt the dog's back as it whimpered in pain. She tried to soothe it with shushing sounds. "Back feels fine. I don't think there're any breaks." She ran her hands along the dog's side. "Ribs, hmm not sure." Then she moved on to its head, shining a light into each eye. The animal was surprisingly cooperative. "Her head doesn't look so good. She could have a concussion. I better keep her here for a while. It's amazing she wasn't hurt worse."

"Yeah, he kicked her pretty hard."

"Who did this?" she asked as she continued to feel the dog's bones. "Oh my, her leg maybe... Hmm."

"What?"

"Nothing, go on," Aunt Vicki said, frowning in thought.

"It was Brian."

She stopped to glare at Jay. "You're kidding me. What's wrong with that kid? Why did he hurt a poor, defenseless dog?"

"It's a long story."

"You'll have to tell me about it tonight. This is unacceptable. I won't allow it," she snapped, her voice sharp with fury. "I'm done with this. That kid is driving me straight over the edge."

As Aunt Vicki continued to examine the dog, Jay noticed its tags were facing him. "Nina," he read aloud. Aunt Vicki's head snapped in his direction at the name. The dog followed suit, only in slow motion. "What?" he asked defensively, his eyes darting between them.

"What did you say?"

"Just reading the tag. *Nina. 3535 Mercy Lane.*"

"Jay, I want you to go home," Aunt Vicki commanded, her voice quivering.

"What did I do?"

"You didn't do anything, honey. It would be best if you went on home so I can focus my attention on her, and she can get some space."

Jay quickly went from defensive to angry. "You can focus on her while I'm here and I'm doing nothing to her space."

"Jay, please. I can't handle this distraction."

"I don't want to. I need to learn this stuff if I'm ever gonna do what you do someday."

"Jay..."

Something inside him wanted to stay near Nina, to take care and protect her, and he dug his heels in. "I want to make sure she's okay."

"She'll be okay. I'll take good care of her. I promise."

"I just want to be sure."

"Please do as I say," Aunt Vicki snapped, her voice laced with anger, refusing him eye contact. None of this was making any sense. Why were her hands shaking?

"What's wrong?"

She tightened her mouth in frustration. "You're not listening. Do I have to talk to your dad about your behavior?"

"Fine." Jay stomped to the exit in a huff. That was pretty low, bringing Dad into it.

"Don't be mad, Jay. It's nothing personal."

Ignoring her, he swung open the door and headed past the counter to the front, whispering under his breath. "Yeah, nothing personal, Jay" he mocked. "But I don't want you around." What a joke.

"How's the doggie?" Miss Connie asked, working hard to remove a spot on the floor with her mop. "Is it okay?"

"I wouldn't know." Jay passed her by, glancing back only for a second. "If I were you, I wouldn't go back there. Aunt Vicki's having a meltdown."

Miss Connie's face scrunched in confusion as Jay disappeared through the door. "That kid has lost his mind," he heard her say as it closed behind him.

He figured Brian was probably at the ER by now, but he booked it home just in case. He never knew who he might run into—literally. His legs burned with every step as anger boiled inside him.

If only Nina's owners would have kept her locked up and safe, none of this would have happened. "Jerks," he muttered with disdain. He'd love to knock on their door and tell them what a-holes they were.

As he came to the end of Mercy Lane and rounded

the corner to his cul-de-sac, he stopped at the last house on the street. "3535 Mercy Lane," he reminded himself. The lowest number on Mercy Lane was 3537. Jay stood there staring at the address, out of breath and confused. "If it stops at 3537, where is 3535?" he asked himself, scanning the houses.

Then it hit him. There was no 3535 Mercy Lane.

9

WISH YOU WERE HERE

Aunt Vicki brought a large, freshly prepared bowl of spaghetti to the table where Jay and his dad sat on opposite ends. Jay had been dying to know how the dog was but felt uncomfortable bringing it up in front of Dad. Knowing him, he would turn it around and start drilling Jay with questions, of which he was in no mood. However, after five minutes of sitting on his hands, the suspense got the best of him. "How's Nina?" he asked as Aunt Vicki leaned in to scoop noodles onto his plate. She jumped, nearly flipping the entire bowl into his lap. That would have sucked. He backed his chair up a bit to be on the safe side.

"Who's Nina?" Dad asked. Did Jay know his dad or what?

"A dog at the Humane Society," Jay answered without taking his eyes off Aunt Vicki. "She okay?"

"Yep. She'll be just fine." Aunt Vicki served Dad his food before serving herself.

Dad sneezed and sniffed miserably. He was even allergic to *conversations* about dogs. "How did this dog get hurt?" He let out another sniffle, this one long and juicy as he slathered butter onto his bread.

Aunt Vicki answered for him as she pulled up her chair. "Jay brought the dog to me because Brian kicked the poor thing." Jay shot a goaded look her way. Why did she have to bring up Brian?

Dad took a bite of bread, looking puzzled. "Who?" he asked between chews.

Aunt Vicki cleared her throat as she stabbed at her salad. "You know, the kid who gave Jay the black eye."

Dad stopped in mid-chew, pushing up his smudged glasses as if that, instead of a good cleaning, would give him a clearer vision of Jay sitting across from him. "That punk kid bothering you again?"

"It's nothing, really," Jay insisted.

"This kid's torturing animals now?"

"It's whatever. Can we not make it a thing?"

"Torture? Okay." Shaking his head in disbelief, Dad sipped his iced tea and set the glass down with a smack of his lips. "Anyway, I guess that's why his mother called and asked if you had a dog."

Jay raised his eyebrows. "She did?"

"Yeah, Vicki talked to her." Dad said, his mouth full, gesturing at her with his forehead. "I wondered why she asked about a dog. Of course, she told her you don't have one."

Jay turned his attention to Aunt Vicki. "Did you tell her about Nina?"

"No."

"Why not?"

She shook her head, keeping her eyes down at her salad. "She was pretty angry, and I honestly didn't feel like it was worth arguing about."

"If that boy hurt a dog, you should have told his mom, Vicki. The nerve of some people." Dad nodded at Jay. "You know, I should call his father and tell him what that thug is doing." He took another bite, acting like he'd just come up with something so brilliant it was sure to teach somebody, somewhere, a lesson they would never forget.

"No, don't," Jay said in monotone, not worried. Dad was all talk. "You might actually have human contact with someone, and you wouldn't want that."

Dad froze in mid-chew, and Jay could only imagine the look he was surely flashing him. Jay didn't meet his gaze. Instead, he stared at his plate, twirling his noodles round and round on his fork with no real intention of eating them, all while attempting to shrink himself down to the smallest possible size.

"Jay!" Aunt Vicki snapped. "Not nice."

"Watch how you speak to me, Jay." Dad pointed his fork at him with accusation. "Not too bright for a kid as smart as you to speak that way to someone who has the power to ground you for a month."

He was right, and Jay hated it.

"You need a better set of friends," Dad continued, getting another forkful of noodles.

"Any friends would be great at this point." Jay dropped his fork onto his plate with a sharp clink, sulking as the sound echoed in the tense silence.

"What about Ishmael?" Aunt Vicki suggested. "He's perfectly nice."

Jay rolled his eyes at the mention of this name. "That's the problem with him, though. He's perfect. Or at least he thinks he is."

She clicked her tongue. "Why do you say that? He seems like a good kid."

"Sure, but you never had to spend any actual *time* with him. That was like the worst three Thursdays of my life. I still can't believe you made me do that."

"Oh, for gosh sake. Not exaggerating at all, are we?" Aunt Vicki shoved a bite of salad into her mouth, giving him a crooked smile as she chewed. "If you want my opinion, I don't think you gave him much of a chance," she added after she swallowed, then took a gulp of iced tea as Jay rolled his eyes again. She had no idea. "I mean, think of it, Jay. You're both home-schooled, you're both about the same age, and you're both bright kids. You could be the perfect friends."

Aunt Vicki was incorrect on three counts. The facts were that one: Ishmael wasn't the same age as Jay. He was a year younger. Two: Ishmael was about a billion times smarter. In fact, saying they were, "both bright kids," was like comparing a penlight to the sun. And lastly: Jay hadn't given him a chance at all.

Ishmael lived three houses down across the cul-de-sac from them. He'd always been home-schooled. In fact, Aunt Vicki said he'd never stepped one foot into a school building his entire life. He was an only child and lived with just his mom, a woman named Usha Shetty.

Aunt Vicki had met Usha Shetty at the Humane Society when she'd lost track of their highly sophisticated, long-haired cat named Myra. Aunt Vicki had somehow gotten it into her brain that it would be a good idea if Ishmael and Jay got together and became the best friends ever. But that wasn't to be.

Ishmael Robinson. Man, that guy was a jerk. From the instant he'd opened his lips, that were way too red and wet not to be an annoying distraction, he had bugged him. Jay could have predicted what kind of time he was going to have the minute he stepped into the kid's neat, tidy, color coordinated bedroom on that first Thursday Aunt Vicki made Jay spend the afternoon with him. His bookshelves were lined perfectly straight with about a bajillion nice, new-looking hardbacks. Butterflies were pinned to boards, trophies on display on shelves and bugs in man-made habitats.

"Do you want to see my codes?" That was the first thing out of his mouth. Not, "Hi." Not, "How are you?" Not, "Tell me about yourself," which was not only not his first sentence, but never escaped his shiny lips at all, ever. "I'm fantastic at cracking codes. I can crack any code. Any! You can try me on that. I can even read almost any language if you give me long enough. I'm the best in the world. The world champion, in fact." Jay wasn't aware a cracking code competition even existed and yet, somehow, this Ishmael kid was the world champion. Unreal.

All the guy did was brag. He bragged about his grades, his mother being some sort of inventor, his IQ, and how many languages he knew fluently including French, Spanish, Arabic, and Hindi (his mother's native tongue). It went on and on. If Ishmael wasn't incessantly talking about himself, he wasn't happy. Unfortunately for him, there was nothing in the universe Jay cared about less.

Ever since Ishmael had moved into the neighborhood

about a year ago, he'd waved at Jay every time he saw him, although never with even a hint of a smile. However, since the last of the Thursday afternoon 'play dates,' (as Jay sarcastically called them) all he ever got was an immediate back of the head or the occasional look that could kill.

Just the other day, Ishmael and Miss Usha were in their driveway unloading groceries from their car. Jay had caught Ishmael's eye and waved with apprehension. Ishmael had smoothed back his dark hair from his face and stared at Jay with zero emotion. The lenses in his oversized glasses on his pinhead glared in the light, making him look like a part fly, part boy creature. Super-fly. *That would make a great nickname*, Jay thought. He'd never say it to his face, of course, but strictly behind his back, which was the only polite thing to do.

"Not sure what happened," Aunt Vicki continued, "but Usha won't answer my phone calls."

Jay felt bad for what had happened about a month and a half ago, the last time he'd talked to Ishmael. He could fill her in on it and clear up the mystery for her, but he wouldn't dare. She'd lose it on him for sure.

"Usha." Dad pursed his lips in thought. "She's the Indian woman, right?"

"Yeah, Usha Shetty a few doors down," Aunt Vicki replied as she moved food around on her plate.

"I remember you mentioning her. Single mom?" Dad wiped the spaghetti sauce off his chin with a worn out napkin.

"Yep. I guess they never got married. She never told me much about her ex except that they had a lot of issues because of their different religions. He was a Muslim I guess."

Jay had enough of Ishmael talk and wasn't about to let Aunt Vicki avoid the subject of Nina. "Did you find any broken bones?"

"What?" She turned to him with a puzzled expression.

"Did Nina have any bones broken?"

"Oh, no. She's okay. She'll just be sore for a while. Don't worry about her." She waved him off. "Really, she's fine."

"I don't get how that's possible." Jay frowned, hoping she'd provide him eye contact, but she didn't. Aunt Vicki was hiding something, and he wasn't going to let it go until he found out what.

"Well, it is."

"Where's she now?"

"I, um." She cleared her throat. "I sent her home," she mumbled, squirming in her seat.

"Her owners came in?"

"Jay, can we talk about this later?"

"Who are the owners?"

She pressed her lips together, examining her plate with a frown. "I'm done talking about work, okay?"

"I just want to know about her owners. I mean, they let Nina out with, like no leash every day. Did you yell at them?" He wanted to bring up the address, but not in front of Dad.

Dad piped in, "Jay, stop giving her the third degree, for God's sake. She said, she doesn't want to talk about it."

"But none of it makes sense. I just—"

"Jay!" Dad pounded the table hard enough to make the silverware clink, his jaw clenched. "Cut it."

Jay slumped in his seat, angry at being dismissed like... well, like a dog. He was so ticked off that he didn't feel guilty at all for what he did next.

JAY BREATHED IN THE EVENING AIR, FEELING A TWINGE OF déjà vu. He loved the smell of the night and the coolness of it. It reminded him of the time he'd spent with his family on the fourth of July back when Dad was normal, he still had his mom, and he'd felt happy and hopeful.

The memory faded little by little as the years went by —the three of them together, his mom holding him tight as they all sat on a blanket in the grass amongst hundreds of other people, waiting for the fireworks to start. He remembered what she smelled like, a mixture of soap and perfume.

It had been so long, and he'd been so young, only three years old. Maybe some of those memories were just dreams in his mind, he wasn't sure. "How could you possibly remember any of that? You were just a baby." Dad would say. But he did remember some things.

He recalled how she used to give him hugs, cover his face in kisses, how it made him feel so safe. She would call him her "little man" and comb his hair nice and straight. The sound of her hearty laughter could make him smile and giggle, even if he wasn't privy to the reason behind it.

With a heavy heart, he thought about how he'd never hear it again, never smell her perfume or feel her arms around him. Worse than that, he had a difficult time picturing her face outside of the one photo he had of her. Those days with Mom were gone forever, leaving only vague memories and feelings.

He reached down and grabbed the chain around his neck, rubbing his nail over Mom's ruby ring that hung from it. Jay hadn't taken the necklace off since Dad let him wear it. It was his very most prized possession. When he held the ring in his fist, he always felt closer to her. Something about it helped him feel better when he was sad. "Wish you were here," he whispered, gripping it tight.

Jay hadn't snuck outside to reminisce. He'd come out for a different reason, and he needed to stop feeling sorry for himself and get to it.

He was still grounded from his bike, but by the time he got back, no one would ever notice he'd left. Aunt Vicki had already finished the dishes and was in the guesthouse getting ready for bed. Dad was in his den watching TV and messing with his laptop. Jay was on his own for the rest of the night and glad for it.

After kicking off the kickstand, he jumped onto his bike and pedaled out of the cul-de-sac into the creepy, quiet darkness. Even though he was getting the willies, the kind that ran down your backbone, he pressed forward until Lydia's house came into view. Again, a bunch of loud, angry words spewed from her home. He felt bad she had to deal with that all the time. That had to seriously suck.

He laid the bike down in her neighbor's yard and crouched behind some hedges by the sidewalk to hide. Nighttime noises of bugs chirping filled the air along with the occasional car driving past, headlights briefly cutting through the darkness, only to fade away into the quiet again. After about five minutes, he saw what he'd expected. He had set a trap to get the answers he wanted, and it had worked.

Across the street, from inside some bushes, a pair of eyes glowed in the darkness, reflecting off the porch light behind him. But he wasn't afraid. He knew exactly who they belonged to.

10

WITHOUT A LEASH

Vicki lay sprawled out on the couch reading a mystery thriller in her pink robe, her feet in matching fuzzy slippers resting on the coffee table. Just as the plot was taking a shocking turn, a pounding on the door made her bolt upright.

"Who could that be?" Before all four words escaped her lips, Jay called out her name.

"Aunt Vicki!"

"Jay?" The sound of his voice was concerning. "You okay? Hold on!" She ran to the door, unlocked the deadbolt and flung it open quickly. "What's wrong?"

"You let the dog go," Jay accused her, out of breath. "You didn't give her to her owners. You just let her go!"

Vicki clicked her tongue softly and let out the air she'd been holding in her lungs.

"Nina's alone out there in the dark, probably still hurt. And you," he motioned to her with an open palm, "who usually cares more about animals than anyone I know, let her loose to live on the street." He looked angry enough to cry. "Why, Aunt Vicki?"

"What are you talking about, Jay? Shouldn't you be in bed?" She tightened the belt of her robe securely around her waist, wishing he would let it go. Knowing him, he'd persist until she provided an explanation that satisfied him, which she was unable to do.

"I need to know."

"Get in here." She tugged his arm, dragging him inside before slamming the door. "Your dad will be out here any minute wondering what the heck's happening."

"He won't be the only one."

"Jay, please."

"I saw the dog. I saw Nina."

"Where?"

"Why? Does it matter? I saw her outside without a leash in the same place I always see her."

"When? Tonight?"

"A few minutes ago." Jay shook his head, anger and disbelief on his face. "You know she's there!"

"What were you doing down the street? Your dad would have a coronary."

Jay didn't seem to care he was breaking the rules. He had no fear of her. No doubt, she'd been too lenient with him over the years. "Why did you let her go? She's hurt." The look on his face was heart wrenching, and she wished she could say something to reassure him.

She tried to keep her voice steady and calm, although inside she was anything but. "Like I've told you a few times now, she's okay. I wouldn't have released her if she wasn't."

"That's another thing. How's that even possible? Brian whacked her against a wall and kicked her. She could barely even move when I brought her to you."

"I know. But she is fine. I promise."

"Fine? Doesn't it bother you she's never on a leash? That her owners don't take care of her? I don't get it!" Jay waved his hands around in anger, not accepting any of it.

Vicki couldn't blame him. "Jay."

"You always get so mad when people don't leash their dogs. Remember that one time that dog got hit by a car?"

"Yes, but—"

"Don't you care that it might happen again—to Nina?"

There was no way to explain this to him and she desperately wished he would just take her answer as is. "I know her owners."

"So, if you know them personally it's okay for them to abuse animals?"

The kid had some good points. All she could do was give vague answers and hope they would suffice until she came up with something better. "Jay, they don't abuse animals. Nina's not in danger."

"Then who are they?" Jay crossed his arms. "Who are her owners?"

"It's late, Jay. You need to go take your shower and get ready for bed." She put her hand on his shoulder, and he shrugged her off, fuming.

"I want to know."

"I'm sorry, Jay. There are some things we can't talk about."

He let his hands fall at his sides in frustration, and his voice turned into a whine she'd heard many times over the course of his life. "Since when can't we talk about a dog? It's just a dog!" In most cases, that would work, but this time it couldn't.

"You'll have to trust me, okay?"

The whining continued, as if he thought laying it on thicker would be more effective. "But Aunt Vicki—"

"I mean it, Jay."

"It's impossible! She can't be well enough to be out there on her own."

"Jay—"

"Not after being kicked! Not after being slammed up against a wall!"

"Stop making things bigger than they are."

"Aunt Vicki!" he screamed, grabbing her attention. "There is no 3535 Mercy Lane!"

She was quiet for a second before speaking softly. "What do you mean?"

"On Nina's collar, the tag said 3535 Mercy Lane. I checked and there's no 3535 on Mercy Lane."

Vicki lost her breath. Of course, they would use an address that didn't exist. And of course, Jay would investigate. She should have known. "Maybe you read it wrong."

"No, I didn't. I'm telling you the truth."

"Well, I don't know." Vicki ran her fingers through her hair nervously, not sure where to go from here. He'd stumped her.

"Where do they live? You said you knew them. What's their address?"

"I don't want to talk about this."

He threw his hands out helplessly. "I don't get you."

"I know, Jay," she told him with sincere remorse in her voice. "I'm sorry."

"Make it make sense."

"Jay—"

"You always say that I can talk to you about anything. But you can't talk to me?"

"Why aren't you listening to me? What would your mother say?" Vicki asked, immediately raising her fingers to her mouth. Why had she said that? It had come out of nowhere and spilled out of her before she was able to stop it.

However, her insensitive remark didn't seem to faze Jay at all. He was beyond angry. "She'd probably say you're acting crazy and ask you if you took your pills today." He turned away and rolled his eyes.

"Jay!" Vicki exclaimed, then her shoulders slumped slightly, and she frowned with irritation. "Crap. I did forget to take my pills today." She marched off to the bathroom with Jay at her heels.

"I don't understand why you're acting this way. I mean, it's not like you."

Vicki popped open a bottle, shook out a yellow pill and swallowed it dry, making a face. "Just know I have my reasons. I'm not saying anything else about it, so let it drop for now." She placed a hand on her chest with a pained expression.

"You should probably drink water with that," he suggested.

"Thanks," she said with sarcasm. "Go home and we'll discuss this another time." She grabbed his arm lightly and led him to the front door.

"Tomorrow?"

"Probably not. But, another time, I promise."

"You're killing me," Jay told her as he stepped out into the night.

She closed the door. "Ditto, kid. I love you, but ditto." Quickly, she opened it again. "Night, sweetie. I love you very much." Then she closed it, thankful she'd been able to sidestep the conversation. For now.

11

POWERLESS OR WEAK

Vicki raked her hands through her short hair, combing it with her fingers to make it at least halfway presentable, unsure why since no other visitors would grace her doorstep tonight.

Her cat, Scarlet, emerged from the shadows to jump onto her lap. As Vicki stroked her silver fur, a frown overtook her face, a tangle of concerns running through her mind. Jay was getting older, and more questions were sure to pop up. It had never been easy answering his inquiries about his mother, and the answers were becoming harder and harder to come up with.

Her thoughts traveled to Jay's mom, her dear sister. How she missed Tara. She loved her so much that she'd given up her life, the one Tara had saved from certain death, in service to her. But although Tara's family had been such a blessing, all her secrets were a burden. How much longer could she bear it?

And yet, Vicki had her own secrets—lots of them. Before she knew it, a small smile came over her face as she studied the shiny red stone on her finger. The large gem in its setting sparkled more than any stone on this earth. Even after all these years, the force it contained still amazed her. She must have looked at it about a hundred times a day, and still it was as if seeing it for the very first time. Its power was subtle yet alive, and she learned how to harness and master it more and more each day. "Paragon," she whispered. That's what they called it now.

With a loud exhale, she contemplated her secrets. Hiding them for so many years had almost driven her mad. She could answer all of Jay's questions in just one conversation: Why his father had become so antisocial, so agoraphobic—this was her fault, and to her dismay, there was nothing she could do about it now. Why she didn't allow Jay to have a cell phone—so no one would be able to trace him. Why she took him out of public school —if he ever found out that she'd set him up to get suspended so she could keep him safe at home, he would never speak to her again. The truth about what had happened to his mother—although she herself didn't have the full story, she had her suspicions. She could explain it all and more, but she wouldn't dare.

What about her own history? If she shared it with him, he wouldn't even believe her. It would be too much for his brain to comprehend or accept.

And now she had this dog to contend with. She knew where it had come from. The name and its collar had given it away. If she didn't already have enough guilt, seeing the creature left her with even more regret. "What was I thinking?" What she wouldn't give to go back in time. She could kick herself for allowing David to talk her into getting involved in his ridiculous dog plan.

"What should I do, Scarlet?" she asked her companion. "I need to figure out why Nina's following Jay." David was up to something. There was no doubt about that.

She had no interest in returning to her book, even though she was at the good part. She had a lot of thinking to do. There were plans to be made.

JAY HAD PLANS OF HIS OWN. HE WAS BOUND AND determined to find out what was going on between Aunt Vicki and the dog. Because something was going on. He knew it. There was something he was missing, and he was going to figure it out. And once he made up his mind, he wasn't one to let it go.

But his plan wasn't working. Trying to sneak up on Nina was like trying to catch a fly in his fist. Some way, somehow, this dog appeared to know where he was before he even knew himself. Over the next few days, he had seen her a few times in her regular spot, but always when he approached, she disappeared as if in mid-air.

After four days of this, he was left frustrated and hopeless and had all but given up. But that afternoon, he had a thought. "How did I catch her last time?" he asked himself, reasoning, deducing. "She rescued me." Would she rescue him again? It seemed to be his only hope.

He took his sweet time on the way to the Humane Society. Lydia typically walked home from school around 3:20 to 3:30 and, although he always tried to avoid her, today he would be sure to be halfway between her home and the school at that time. "With my luck, she'll be home sick or something."

But she wasn't. He spotted her walking with a girl-friend toward him. Her friend had bright blonde hair with black roots and was aggressively gnawing on a wad of gum, her shiny pink lips working in overdrive with the effort as her thumbs moved at the speed of light across her phone. Brian wasn't in sight.

"Meat eaters are carnivores, right?" Lydia asked her.

"Yeah, I think so," the blonde replied between chews without looking up. By the looks of her, it was surprising she could walk, talk, text and chew gum all at the same time.

"The plant eaters are herbivores. So, what do you call animals that eat both meat and plants?"

"Um." The girl moved her glossy lips to the right side of her face, her brain working in overdrive. Then she perked up, enlightened. "Omnipotent!"

Lydia frowned. When she spotted Jay, her eyes grew wide. "Hey!"

He glanced behind him as if to question who she was talking to.

"Jay!" she clarified with annoyance.

"Yeah?" They stopped to face one another.

Lydia's frown reappeared as she shifted her weight, popping out a hip and planting a hand on it. Jay fought to keep his expression neutral, although his knees were knocking. "You know, Brian had to get, like treated for rabies because of your stupid dog!"

He wanted to laugh but suppressed it, knowing better. Rabies, he'd heard, was painful to treat. If what Lydia said was true, Brian ought to be in rare form the next time he saw him. "That's dumb. It doesn't have rabies. Besides, it's not my dog, anyway."

"Right. If it's not your dog," she mocked, "then how do you know?"

"You can just tell. It wasn't foaming at the mouth or acting weird."

"Well, they couldn't find it, so they're not taking any chances. And when Brian's mom called your aunt, she lied for you and said it isn't your dog."

"She didn't lie. It isn't my dog."

"Please. Don't make up lies to save yourself. Brian isn't stupid."

Yeah, right. Jay wanted to say this out loud, but what would be the point? "Where is he anyway?"

"He's at home recovering today. You're lucky he ain't here." Jay supposed he was lucky, although he needed Brian to trap the dog. Now he'd have to find another way. "He's about sick of being screwed over by you. Now he's gotta get shots for like two weeks."

"I did nothing to him." He couldn't have cared less about Brian. However, he didn't care much for Lydia standing there yelling at him. It hurt. Especially after she'd done him the kindness of returning his cap, revealing her true feelings. Now she was ticked off at him. Talk about mixed signals.

Unable to meet her angry gaze for long, he turned to the blonde, who hadn't glanced up from her phone the entire time they'd been standing there. "Omnivores is the word you're looking for," he told her, and she lifted her head, a crease forming between her narrowed brows.

"What?" She continued to chomp aggressively on her gum as she snarled at him.

"Omnivores are both plant and meat eaters," he explained to Lydia, then turned back to the blonde. "Omnipotent means all powerful or invincible."

"Whatever," blondie mumbled with no interest, rolling her eyes. "Stalker."

Out of nowhere, two large male figures appeared on either side of him. *Crap.* The blonde gum-gnawer cackled as Smith and Thad each grabbed one of his arms and lifted him up with very little effort, carting him over to the side of a fence behind a large patch of brush. No one could see him here, not even the dog if she ever showed up, as he was too far away from her usual spot. *All part of the plan,* he tried to tell himself, his heart racing.

"You know what the opposite of omnipotent is?" Smith barked as he yanked Jay up by the front of his collar. He was beginning to be accustomed to being jerked around this way. Maybe they'd all watched a YouTube video called, *How to Rough Up a Nerdy Kid Who's Much Smaller Than You by Yanking on His Clothing Until He is Nearly Strangled.* "Dead!" he roared, shoving his wide, flat, freckled nose into Jay's face.

"Actually," Jay choked out, "the opposite would be—"

"Shut up!" Smith's melon head was large and red with anger—to the exploding point.

"You mess with Brian, you mess with us. Got it?" Thad joined in.

The only thing Jay understood was together, the two of them didn't equate to half a brain.

"I said, you got it?"

Smith shook him again until he answered. "Yes," Jay was so frustrated with himself for screwing up his own plan that he barely noticed the humiliation once again being inflicted upon him. Out of the corner of his eye, he caught Lydia and her friend standing nearby along with several kids congregating around them. A few of them filmed him with their phones. "Powerless or weak," he whispered.

"What did he say?" Thad asked.

That's what Jay was. "The opposite of omnipotent."

"Seriously? I told you to shut up, you clown!" Smith growled, tightening his grip.

He wished he could vanish into thin air like Nina seemed to. If Smith would only let him go, he would run down the sidewalk to get closer to the dog's usual spot. He could even run slower than he was capable of and still get away, yet lure Smith and Thad into the chase with the ruse they'd be able to catch him. Then maybe Nina would show up. But was all of that worth it?

"Okay, Gay," Thad bellowed.

Jay turned his focus his way although Smith had forced his chin up in a most uncomfortable position, which made even the slightest eye movement painful.

"Where's your dog?"

Jay hoped one of the many white heads that decorated Thad's angry, red face wouldn't burst with the pressure and squirt him in the eye, or worse. He closed his mouth tight, nauseated by the thought. "It's not mine," he choked out.

Smith shook him, harder this time. "We're not playing your stupid games. Where is it?"

"I don't know." Jay had a hard time breathing and wished they would just beat him up and get it over with.

Seeming to read his mind, Thad balled up his fist. "Fine. Brian asked us to give you a little present."

Smith flashed his off-white, crooked teeth in a large, sinister grin. "Time to add more bruises to your ugly face." He and Thad both raised their white-knuckled fists. As soon as he felt Smith release him, Jay didn't wait for his deflated lungs to fill with air before ducking between their arms to make his getaway.

Smith quickly stuck out his thick foot and Jay tripped right over it. He attempted to use his hands to brace himself from the fall. Still, the right side of his face hit the concrete. He lay there, still as stone, hearing laughter from behind him. *Well, that didn't work.* That was the last thought he had before the pain hit him. His whole face, the side that was still healing, ached with a throbbing so fierce, he had to hold back the tears he couldn't shed in front of the jerks standing above him.

As he writhed in pain, he closed his eyes tight, listening to Smith and Thad's taunting. "Idiot," one of them mumbled.

Through all the laugher, Jay heard a barking, which made him sit up fast. Too fast. The sudden movement caused his head to spin almost to the point of being unbearable. Black spots formed in his vision.

"The dog!" Smith screamed out. "That's Jay's stupid dog!"

"Where?" Thad said.

"There!"

"Let's get it!" Chaos erupted. Everyone was screaming, running, and before long, he was alone. He scrambled to his feet, watching maybe ten kids dart into a patch of woods off the road. The dog was steering them away. Nina had saved him again.

"Dang, that dog is fast," a voice uttered nearby.

"Super fast," another said.

Jay recalled people saying the same thing about him when he was in track at school. It was time for him to become super fast himself, although it would help if the earth would stop spinning for a moment.

A big splotch of red appeared on the light gray concrete below him. It wasn't until he reached up to touch his nose that he realized it was gushing blood. No time to worry about it. Nina was leading them on a goose chase, and Jay knew better than to follow it as the others had. He knew where to go.

He snatched his cap, which had fallen off in the struggle, threw it back on and ran, pinching his nose and tripping on his own feet, resembling a drunk with a nosebleed. "I have to get there," he told himself with a nasal tone. "Have to!"

Soon, Lydia's house came into view from across the street. He dove behind some bushes and peeked out in all directions, trying to keep as quiet as possible. Seconds later, the black dog appeared behind him in Lydia's neighbor's lawn. She actually seemed to be tiptoeing while scanning the area around her. *What are you up to, dog?* Jay wondered as he wiped the blood off his nose with the back of his hand.

He watched as she used her snout to lift a small, rectangular, plastic cover in the grass. It was of the same color green, camouflaging it rather neatly. After slipping inside, she nudged the cover back over the hole with her nose like she'd done it a million times.

Intent on following her, he leapt out of the bushes. "3535 Mercy Lane." He'd found it. "This is it. This is where she lives."

He opened the lid to peer down into the darkness. Though he couldn't see a thing, he heard her moving. Skinny as he was, he still wasn't sure he would fit. He rubbed his tight chest. Maybe he was claustrophobic.

Remembering, he patted his left pocket. "The flashlight." Dad had put it on his key chain because he kept losing his key. He flicked it on and shined it down to find her gone. "Wow, you *are* super fast."

The light revealed several rusty rungs jutting out of the wall. At the bottom, a patch of dirty water glistened, and the pipe appeared to curve so nothing else was visible beyond that point. Just thinking about going down had him on the verge of hyperventilating. Yet if he didn't hurry, she would get away.

"Uh." He grunted as he knelt beside the hole. An unpleasant moldy smell combined with something like rotten eggs hit his senses, taking away his ability to breathe. How did the dog get down this thing? It seemed impossible. "I can't do this." He gagged. "I can't."

"It went this way," someone announced from behind him.

"Crap." He whipped around and shoved both feet inside. Instantly, they went cold. It must have been twenty degrees cooler inside. He climbed down the slippery metal rungs and got so far that only his head was out. It was snug—too snug. "I'm not even gonna fit." He didn't think he could be more frightened than he was, at least not until the voices grew louder.

"Where is that stupid dog?" Thad asked from somewhere close by.

As fast as possible, Jay threw the cover on top of him and ducked into the blackness, his heart burning inside his chest. "Crap!" he muttered again, fidgeting with his light and shining it downward. The dark, concrete walls surrounding him were so close, he feared he might start freaking out. "Okay, I'll stay here for a few more minutes until I'm sure they're gone." He took a deep, cleansing breath before remembering the air was vile and coughed silently. "It's okay. It's cool."

His foot slipped underneath him, and he frantically grabbed onto another rung to avoid free falling to the bottom. In his effort, he dropped the flashlight. It made a soft tink as it landed below, turning off on impact, leaving him in the darkness, the only light coming from a hole about the size of a dime on the cover. "No!" he screamed in a whisper.

"What was that?" Thad asked from above him.

"Unbelievable," Jay whispered under his breath as the beam of light above his head disappeared. Someone stood directly above him, covering the small hole and taking away his only light source.

He climbed down carefully to retrieve his flashlight in the pitch black, scrambling for the rungs in his blindness. Once he got going, it became a lot easier to maneuver down, and the hole widened as he went. He was glad to get some distance between the surface and himself, afraid Thad and Smith would lift the cover and find him cowering inside and pull him out by his hair.

Once at the bottom, he almost face planted again, but managed to stay on his feet with his hands extended to brace himself against the wall. After feeling around on the wet floor, his fingers found the keys. "Hurry! Hurry!" he pled with himself, desperate, fearing he might not be alone. To his surprise and relief, the flashlight came back on after shaking it up and down a few times. Sure that he would find a cryptic face glaring at him from some nook or cranny, he shined it around, finding nothing but a pipe leading off to the left.

The adjacent pipe was large and round, and he ducked into it, taking a deep lungful of the damp, rank air, feeling the walls might swallow him up. He lifted his flashlight to find the dirty, moldy pipe curved to the right ahead.

Jay followed the pipe, unsure of what he might find. As he peeked around the corner, a small, dark figure disappeared around a curve. "Nina." He was hot on the dog's trail, about to find out where Nina had been hiding. Finally.

12

TUNNELS

J ay found himself ankle deep in water, hoping to God it wasn't sewage. Although it was pretty gross, he assumed the smell would be worse if it was. Still, it was disturbing to trudge around in water, not knowing what was in it.

To steady himself, he braced a hand against the grimy, rusted wall of the pipe that enclosed him, yanking it back when he felt a wet, slimy substance. "Nasty!" He wiped the brownish-green grunge on the butt of his jeans and picked up the pace, desperate to reach the end of this eerie, dark trail and perhaps get somewhere a little less disgusting. Regardless, he'd decided he would follow the dog all night long if he had to in whatever conditions lie ahead, no matter how dangerous, gross, or creepy. He'd get his answers if it was the last thing he did.

After turning the corner, he climbed a couple of feet off the ground into the next tunnel. The farther he went, the stronger the stench of rotten eggs became. It hung in the air, thick and suffocating, as though the walls themselves pulsed with the foul odor, stinging his nostrils and making it difficult to breathe.

The narrow tunnel opened into a junction where the path split to the left and right. The new shaft offered a welcome relief, providing far more room to move. Instead of two inches of clearance above him, he had at least three feet and the width had nearly doubled. Jagged rock walls replaced the rusty metal, and the ground was dry and fairly smooth, as if made for travel. As he scanned the area in awe, he wondered who could have carved out such an amazing place.

Unsure which way to go, he shined his light down both passages but saw no sign of the dog in either direction. "Where did you go?" He examined the floor for clues. "That's weird." His voice echoed as he bent to observe bare, wet footprints that led down the tunnel to the right. "Human footprints?" The ground showed no trace of dog prints. Jay realized he was not alone. "Nina *does* have an owner."

With no other choice, he decided to follow the human prints. As an afterthought, he reached down and grabbed a small rock lying at his feet. The thought of being lost somewhere in those tunnels frightened him to the brink of panic, and he wanted to be positive he'd be able to find the way back. He drew an X with it on the rocky wall next to the pipe leading out, just in case.

He walked at a brisk pace, shining his light down the path that seemed to stretch endlessly ahead. The human footprints gradually faded into nothing, and there was no sign of the dog or its owner.

It sounded like cars whizzing by above him indicating he might be directly underneath a road. Though the sound was faint, it could drown out any potential noise, making him vulnerable if someone were to sneak up on him. The thought caused him to pick up his pace.

The beam of his flashlight bounded up and down on the otherwise dark path as he jogged down it. The thought occurred to him that the light he carried might give him away should Nina's owner be lurking around, lying in wait to pounce on him. Not to mention, the key on the chain kept hitting the metal flashlight, making a tinkling noise that amplified and echoed throughout the area. With reluctance, he flicked it off and returned it to his pocket. A small, rectangular, glowing yellow light appeared in the distance. "What's that?" he asked himself, supposing he would know soon enough as he approached it.

Strange hissing noises, accompanied by clicking, came from somewhere in the shadows, making his heart pound like a drum in his chest. As many scary YouTube videos as he had watched, he should know better than to keep going, but his determination to find the dog and to reach what lie at the end of the tunnel overrode his terror. At least for the time being.

With bravery, he continued toward the light. A soft breeze tickled his face and hair, like the kiss of an angel, carrying the damp, earthy scent of a rainforest, quickly followed by the sharp stench of rotten eggs. Goose bumps appeared on his arms as the cool dampness touched his skin.

The hissing grew louder as he approached the light, joined by the wet sounds of chewing and chomping, and a noise like a heavy body being dragged across the ground. He lost his breath for a moment and stopped in his tracks. Unable to tolerate the darkness for a moment longer, he pulled out the flashlight and flicked it on with a shaky finger. The light revealed another intersecting passageway on both sides. The strange sounds seemed to come from inside the pathway on his right. With hesitation, he crept forward and aimed the beam into the darkness. A chill traveled down his spine. Something was very wrong.

When the light reached the source of the noise, his jaw dropped. In the adjacent pathway, an enormous, scaly tail lay swishing from side to side. He trailed the light along its length and revealed the back end of a gigantic crocodile, its massive head shaking as it tore into something with ravenous hunger.

It was too huge to be real. He remembered reading online about a crocodile in an Australian zoo named Elvis, which weighed 1,100 pounds. This one had to be at least twice that size. Gulping down his fear, he restrained himself from turning around in retreat from where he had come. He'd sworn to stop for nothing. But in a million years, he never would've imagined getting eaten by a monstrously large reptile as a possibility.

The yellow glow ahead called out to him, and he knew he couldn't say no to it. The thing hadn't detected him or his light at all, it seemed. Perhaps he could sneak by unseen. But what if it chased him down? Crocodiles were fast runners, and he wouldn't have a prayer to outrun it.

Why am I doing this? He turned the flashlight off and sprinted past the monster, his feet light, concentrating on the faint light ahead to keep from drifting into the wall. *I must be crazy.* The beast's own clamor covered up any noise Jay could ever make. Still, what concerned him most was that it would sense him or smell him. As he ran, he realized he would have to go past it again to get back home. *Wonderful.*

But he couldn't just turn back. Not when he was so very close. As he concentrated on keeping water from escaping his bladder, he tripped over a large rock in his path, using the wall to steady himself. Beyond his control, Jay let out a yelp. The beast silenced its frightful noise as he stood frozen in his tracks. The quiet was way more terrifying than the hissing and chewing had been. Yet, soon enough, it continued making the same racket as loud as ever. Jay let out a very long, silent sigh.

Once he seemed to be in the clear, he began moving again. The noises grew fainter behind him the more distance he put between himself and whatever hellish monster he'd just encountered. Without warning, the light ahead blinked out, leaving only a thin, vertical line. Now finding himself back in near darkness, a sudden sensation of cold sweat hit his body as he panicked, causing him to trip again. This time he fell on his hands, and after that, his knees. Somewhere beside him, he heard squeaking. A man-eating rat, perhaps? The sound spurred him to scramble to his feet even though his palms burned with pain and his kneecaps felt like they might have shifted out of place.

While making his way to the illuminated line of light ahead with his hands outstretched and his knees aching with every step, a soft rattling noise startled him enough to stop. "Crap, not again." What would he find this time? Feeling it safe to turn on his flashlight once more, he fished it out of his pocket.

The rattling grew louder, and a tunnel entrance appeared to the right of the path, as black and uninviting as an entrance into the pit of hell. His light seemed to go on forever inside it, but this time, with relief, he saw no animal of any kind. "Thank God." He blew out a gust of air through puckered lips.

Sudden fear overtook him as he sensed a presence—dark and uninviting. With trepidation, he turned, shining the light on the opposite side of the entrance to reveal a wall covered in scales, a deep shade of sickening green. Traveling upward, he discovered two large yellow eyes that appeared to glow in the dark, each with an eerie, elliptic, cat-shaped pupil. It took a few seconds for his brain to register that the eyes belonged to some kind of morbid, overgrown rattlesnake, which towered several feet above him. Its sleek tongue was so long that it almost touched the top of Jay's head, and its fangs dripped with clear, thick venom.

Jay stifled a scream struggling to escape him. *Its head is bigger than my whole body!* Its eye was larger than two of Jay's spread hands put together! The overly large reptile was looking at him, but not seeing him. Though its tail emitted an ominous rattling, it didn't appear to register Jay was there. It was in some kind of trance.

Realizing he had forgotten to breathe, he gasped for air, spots dancing before his eyes. With careful steps, he crept past the sleeping giant on shaky legs, praying it wouldn't wake before he reached his destination. A few feet away, he broke into a run, terrified something was chasing him—the crocodile, the snake, maybe even a twenty-foot rat (who knew?). He expected something to tackle him and hot fangs to dig into his shoulder blades as he sprinted, shaking so violently he was sure he would drop the flashlight. However, soon enough, he reached the line of light, pivoting quickly to make sure nothing was behind him, knowing there couldn't be. He would have been eaten alive by now if there were.

Turning his attention back to the line of light, he examined it. "It's a door!" he realized, running his hand along the cool rock surface. "There's got to be a handle on this thing somewhere." But there wasn't. He tried pushing it, but it was very heavy. What was he going to do now? There was no way forward, but his heart dropped at the thought of going back. For a fleeting moment, he imagined throwing himself at the stone, as if sheer will might shatter it. But of course, it would do nothing except maybe break his bones.

He let out a shaky breath and rested his forehead against the stone. It was cool against his skin, almost soothing. He closed his eyes, trying to slow his breathing, to think. There had to be something he was missing— some trick, some symbol, some whisper of a clue. He opened his eyes and stepped back again, scanning the edges, the floor, the ceiling. He felt all around the opening. Nothing moved. Nothing gave. But then... something felt different. A rock seemed out of place.

"This is it." He pressed on it as hard as he could, and it shifted, accompanied by creaks of stone against stone which meant... it was moving!

The crack grew larger and larger, until it opened just enough for his thin frame to slip through. He released a gush of air from his lungs, wincing as the stench of rotten eggs grew stronger than ever. Light enveloped him, and he tucked his flashlight back into his pocket, trying to muster the courage to squeeze his way through.

He took a shaky breath, steeling himself. Then, turning sideways, he wedged one shoulder through the gap, feeling the rough stone scrape against his shirt. The space was so tight it pressed against his ribs, and he had to inch forward slowly, twisting and pushing with his legs. His heart hammered in his chest, and for a terrifying moment, he thought he might get stuck. But with a final shove and a grunt of effort, he popped free on the other side, stumbling into the unknown.

Pain distracted him for a moment as he realized he'd scratched a gash on his forearm and had torn off a good bit of skin. He watched the beads of blood appear from the open cut and spread over his arm, cringing as the sting of it hit his brain. He clapped his hand over it as blood dripped onto the ground.

"Hey, you!" a strange, deep, metallic-sounding voice shouted out. Jay's head shot up, and he searched for the source. Of course, he would draw attention from anyone who might be there. With his blood-stained pants ripped open at the knees, a bleeding gash on his arm, a concrete burn on his right cheek along with his black eye and dried blood on his face, how could he not? He must have looked like he'd just returned from war.

"Whoa!" he said as soon as his brain comprehended what his eyes were seeing. He was in a huge cave, lit by flickering flames against the wall and by lampposts scattered about. He caught the faint trickle of running water and the low hum of voices, some distorted and robotic. Gray-colored creatures he had never seen the likes of before wandered around before him along with people.

Some stopped to gawk at him as if he were a strange and freakish thing of nature. All these bizarre sights and sounds overloaded his senses, causing his knees to go weak, and he balanced himself against the cave wall.

He'd stumbled upon a remarkable underground city —another world lurking beneath the surface of the earth. Whatever this place was, it felt alive, welcoming him as if it were waiting for him to find it.

PART II

UNITS AND GRAYS

13

THE GREAT ROOM

S ome sights in this world are so beautiful, they steal your breath, make you 'ooh' and 'ahh,' drop your jaw, or maybe all of the above—like the Grand Canyon, the Northern Lights, or the very first glimpse of the ocean. Yet instantly, Jay became aware everything he'd seen and would see above ground from this point forward would be nothing compared to what he now saw beneath it.

The enormous cave's ceiling rose as high as an enclosed football stadium, and the floor space was almost as vast. A ledge, a few feet higher than the stage, bordered most of the room. Covering much of the wall to his left hung a long, rust-colored curtain draped over what looked like a stage about fifteen feet up. The heavy curtain appeared to be made of small metal chains linked together, with a large symbol woven into its center: an X with two intersecting lines at the bottom, all enclosed in a circle. To Jay, it looked like two crossed swords.

Several paths led to three dark cave entrances, lined with empty golf carts parked along the walls beside them.

He recalled his dad reading an article about stolen golf carts and wondered...

Pots filled with flowers, shrubs, and small trees decorated the trails and peppered the room, perhaps an attempt to make it feel more like the outside. Torches along the walls and scattered lampposts bathed everything in a soft yellow glow. A breeze drifted down from somewhere far above, carrying the scent of fresh air, which made the rancid sulfur smell less overwhelming.

In the middle of it all sat a boulder as tall as a two-story house and about thirteen to fifteen feet wide, spewing out colorful water, lit up by blue, red, yellow, and purple lights. The spectacle would have been gorgeous enough to transfix him, if it wasn't for the beings walking throughout the area, capturing his attention.

That was the freakiest part. Humans roamed about with alien-looking creatures of various heights. Some were short, others tall. The tall ones stood at least six feet, wearing long-sleeved jackets and black boots. Most of the others were much shorter, about half their size, and naked.

They all had the same facial features: gray skin, holes where ears should be, two large, black eyes, two slits for a nose, tiny mouths, and small chins, all on oval-shaped craniums attached to long necks and hairless bodies too thin in proportion to them. Their fingers were long and webbed a quarter of the way up. They looked like typical aliens you would see in almost any sci-fi movie or on websites with stories about alien encounters.

Jay would have turned around and ran like the chicken he was if his legs would have allowed it. In fact, he couldn't move at all. Perhaps it was too late for that, anyway.

"I said, you!" the voice repeated, louder this time. "Respond!" it commanded, in a sound that couldn't possibly have come from a human. Jay located the source —one of the tall creatures dressed in a uniformed jacket and calf-length black boots. It approached him on long legs. Though it used a walking stick that appeared to be made of dark wood, it seemed to float as if on water. The dark-blue jacket covered the skinny arms of the creature, going all the way up its neck and coming down to its waist, leaving its gray, bony legs and its crotch revealed. Thankfully, nothing was there to indicate whether it was male or female.

The creature pointed one of its long fingers at him. "What is your name and number, Unit child?" All of these beings looked the same to Jay. Its deep voice was the only thing to suggest this one might be male.

Jay almost told the creature his name and phone number. The only thing that stopped him was a young girl who came running up to them, her blonde hair bouncing around her head. Out of breath, she told him, "Yag, this is Treb, number 20,426 from up the glacier. He's an acquaintance of mine."

Yag turned his upside down, teardrop-shaped head toward the girl. She was cute, possibly twelve years old, Jay guessed. Her long, golden hair glowed in the dim cave and her blue eyes appeared large on her pale face. The long, peach-colored shirt she wore seemed to be made of burlap or something similar.

With a slow movement, Yag turned back to Jay, examining him. "Why are you here?" he asked with no emotion. "Why are you injured?"

Jay glanced down at his now bloodied hand, still covering the wound on his arm, as the girl answered for him again. "I'm teaching him how to do his assignment, which starts next season." She grabbed Jay's uninjured arm, pulling him closer, and shoved a piece of cloth into his hand. As soon as he realized what it was for, he used it to soak up the blood dripping from his wound.

The commotion attracted more attention, this time from humans nearby, who Jay noticed wore the same type of clothes the girl did in various colors. The girl continued, "He got banged up a bit, but he's okay. Comes with the job, you know." She flashed a crooked grin and laughed nervously.

"Why is he dressed like this?" the thing asked her, pointing his wooden stick at Jay. With judgement in his black, shiny eyes he scanned Jay up and down, noting his Rockies cap along with his dark blue polo shirt and blue jean ensemble before examining his face closely. Jay could see his own reflection in his eyes. The fear in his own expression was intense enough to startle him along with blood on his face from an earlier bloody nose, a concrete burn on his left cheek, and a fading black eye from his fight with Brian. He looked truly awful. Quickly, he snatched the cap from his head, gripping it tight at his chest with both hands.

"He still has his outsider clothes on, that's all." She smiled softly. "He must have forgotten to change."

Yag let out a grunt of disapproval. "We will soon have laws to punish that behavior. You hear me, Unit child?

You Units need more rules, more conformity." He thrust his stick toward Jay's feet. "Show me your ankle."

"M-my ankle?" Jay glanced down at it, wondering if he had yet another injury that he wasn't aware of.

"Yes."

"Yag!" someone close by yelled. Yag rotated toward the voice, which had come from a human-looking man dressed all in black. "Lud has requested you to meet him in the Observation Quarter." The man looked at Jay with intense dark eyes before turning away.

"I am questioning this Unit child."

"Lud said it's urgent," the man yelled over his shoulder with impatience.

Yag grunted as he gravitated to the man and they both made their way to the Observation Quarter, wherever that was. Yag muttered some irritated, unrecognizable words as he tapped his walking stick with each step.

The girl sighed with relief and took hold of Jay's arm again, dragging him down a stone walkway. He followed with no resistance, reveling in the beads of light shining in various colors against the stalactites on the cave's high ceiling. It seemed he was on another planet in some strange galaxy under a foreign sky full of rainbow-colored stars. It was mesmerizing.

She led him into a large tunnel, lit up by a flame in a lamppost. A few feet in, they turned into another one covered by a curtain. This one had a sign next to it. "Majestic," he read, wondering what it meant. The girl swished past the curtain and other curtains in various colors appeared to the right. Colorful designs had been painted on the rock wall next to each one, along with a unique number. The girl stopped in front of a drapery of the same color and fabric as her burlap shirt and nervously scanned the area. He took note of the number: 22898.

"What is a Unit child?" Jay asked. She shushed him and shoved him behind the curtain, joining him inside.

They were in a small rectangular room that was longer than it was wide. The walls were constructed of jagged orange rock, glistening with glittery silver specks. A wooden chair sat next to a stone desk built into the far wall that went across the entire area with books sitting on a shelf above it. A small bed was in the center of the room with a dirty oval rug on the rock floor in front of it.

"Snopes!" The girl balled up her small fists at her sides. "I hope he doesn't check to see if someone named Treb is really in training. I'm sure he's suspicious."

"Suspicious of what?"

"If only I could get to a tele-receiver, then I could warn him..."

"Warn who? Of what?"

She placed a small, white finger to her chin. "But they're all monitored, anyway, just like the CNDs. I'd have to talk in some kind of code, and he might not understand." She sighed, dropping her hand, shaking it off. "Nothing. It's not your worry. I need to get you out of here. But first, can you draw?"

The second best thing Jay was good at, after track, was drawing. He loved it and practiced a lot in his journals. Mostly, he copied other people's creations, and sometimes he sketched the animals at the Humane Society freehand. Once, he even tried to draw Lydia, but her head came out abnormally large and her eyes ended up wonky. "Yes," he answered.

She located a piece of paper on the desk, scribbled something, and tapped her finger on it.

"Draw that," she reached down and pointed to a spot on Jay's left ankle, right above the ball, "right there." She handed him a thin, black marker. "Make it the same size and draw the lines straight." It was identical to the symbol he'd seen on the curtain in the large room, only without the circle around it.

You don't have to be an artist to draw that one, Jay thought. "Why?"

"The mark shows you belong here."

Jay dropped the cloth she'd given him onto the desk-top, his wound beginning to crust over, and bent down to draw the symbol. "What is this place and what are those creatures?"

"Keep your voice down," the girl whispered, grabbing the cloth and dipping it into a pitcher of water on her desk, the water turning a sickening pink. "I realize you don't know me, but please trust me. It's important. We have to get you out of here before we're caught. We're so lucky he didn't have time to look at your ankle. It would've been the end for both of us, for sure. But we're not out of the woods yet. You'll be in tons of trouble if you're caught here in my quarters."

"Sorry if I'm causing problems," he whispered.

"You shouldn't have come here." Her voice was kind, yet Jay could still hear the agitation in it.

Not knowing what to say, he repeated his apology. "Sorry."

It didn't take him long to finish drawing the symbol as she instructed. "Okay that works," she told him, then took the wet cloth and dabbed his face with it until he snatched it from her and finished. "I would fix up your arm, but there's no time. Use that rag to wrap it until you get out of here."

A voice interrupted them from outside the curtain, making them both jump out of their skin. "Time for your Power Lesson." The voice sounded like the same man who had caused the distraction with Yag.

She cleared her throat, trying to regain her composure. "Okay."

"You need to hurry," the man added.

"I will. And, you should know, Treb is training right now." After hearing the man walk away, she looked up in's eyes with seriousness. "Please turn around," she requested in a sweet tone.

"What?"

"I have to get dressed. If I'm late, I'll be in a lot of trouble."

Jay nodded and did as he was told. Less than a minute later, she tapped him on the shoulder, and he turned to face her. She now wore a tight black long-sleeved shirt and black pants, with form-fitting black boots with rubber soles. Her long blonde hair was tied back in a ponytail. She was pretty and petite, about half a foot shorter than him, and younger too, which was easy to forget because she acted so much older.

"Okay." She slung a black leather bag over her shoulder. "We have to go." She took his arm.

"Wait." Jay stopped her. Her ponytail swung around with her and landed on her shoulder as she turned to face him again. "I'm not leaving until you tell me what's going on."

"Please, we haven't much time."

"Then you should probably answer my question so we can go." He crossed his arms, determined to stay put until she spilled her guts.

She took a deep breath through her nose, closing and opening her eyes with impatience.

"I followed a dog into the tunnel that led me here. Do you know what dog I'm talking about?"

She rubbed her lips together and nodded once. "Yes."

"Is it yours?"

She raised her eyebrows. "I'm going to be late."

Jay tightened his crossed arms. "Is the dog yours? I wanna know where it is."

She bit her lower lip before turning away. "I can't answer that."

"Well, you need to. I have to make sure it's okay."

"The dog's safe. I'll answer your questions later, I swear." She twirled around again.

"Wait. I haven't even told you my name."

"I know your name." She sighed. "It's Jay."

Jay frowned at her profile. "How do you know?"

"That's none of your concern."

Jay lifted his brow, his eyes wide. "None of my concern?"

"Seriously, let's go." She peered at him over her

shoulder and pointed to his neck. "By the way, you lost your necklace."

He reached up to his throat and found what she said to be true. "How did you—?"

"Check over where the disgusting pig-boy grabbed you earlier."

Panic hit him at the thought of never seeing the ring again. "I can't lose that necklace. It's very important to me." If he lost it, his only connection to his mother would be gone.

"You'll find it there. Promise." Her voice was soothing and believable, but it did nothing to reassure him. He wouldn't be able to relax until he had it back in his possession and could kick himself for losing track of it. Dad had been right to be reluctant to trust him with it.

Jay frowned. "But, how did you know...?"

"All your questions will have to wait."

"Please, tell me where I am at least."

She glanced up, her expression revealing internal turmoil. "I'll tell you and then we'll go. Promise?"

"Sure, okay."

"This place is called Stoneburrow. And you were in the Great Room, the largest common area."

"Stoneburrow?"

"I'll give you more information later. You promised," she reminded him.

Scenes of the monsters in the tunnels flashed through Jay's mind, making him sweat despite the cold. "Wait," he told her.

"What now?" she whined, slapping her hands to her sides.

"When I came here through the tunnels, there was this huge crocodile. Also, a snake."

She closed her eyes again, throwing her head back as if just remembering. "Oh, yeah." She dropped the leather bag off her shoulder and onto the floor, then bent over it, pulling out two items. She handed them to him, one after the other. First was a flesh-colored fruit about the size of his fist that looked like an artichoke with scales. "Give the crocodile this."

"What is it?" Jay asked while studying it. The shell was hard, like a scaly coconut. He'd never seen anything like it.

"It's enchanted. When you put it before the creature, it will fascinate on it and chew it for at least twenty minutes." Next, she gave him a large gold-colored coin with a hole in the middle and a string attached. "Wave this in the snake's face. After it swings forward and back three times, the snake will fall asleep."

Fear took him over at the mere thought of doing this. "Wave it in its face? As it's biting mine off, maybe?"

"Just do it. Once it sees the coin, it'll stop in its tracks. Don't worry."

"Why is that crocodile and snake in the tunnel? Why are they so huge?"

"They're traps," the girl answered with nervousness.

"Traps?"

"Yes. Now really, let's go."

"You still haven't told me your name."

The girl glanced up at Jay, blinking her large blue eyes, which suddenly seemed strangely familiar. She extended her fist to him, opening it to reveal a blue dog collar. "I'm Nina."

14

TRAPS

Nina dragged Jay through the Great Room by the hand as he moved like a zombie, still in shock as the information just revealed to him slowly sank in. Strange creatures passed him in slow motion, their long, skinny arms swinging at their sides as they took long strides. Their large, dark eyes glared at him as if accurately perceiving he was not part of their world.

According to Nina's instructions, if they were stopped, Jay was to show the symbol he'd drawn on his ankle and everything would supposedly be okay. Luckily, no one paid them too much attention, so it hadn't become necessary.

At the door, she assured him, "I'll see you again and you can ask me all the questions you wish."

"I have lots of questions." He noticed the small scab on the bridge of her nose, which matched the one she had in her dog form. "Especially after what you just told me."

"I'm sure."

"When?"

"Soon. Now, go." She pressed a rock on the wall and the door opened a crack, barely enough for him to squeeze through. Although this time, he didn't scrape himself up, thankfully.

"Oh, and don't tell anyone about me. Nobody," she whispered, peeking through the opening. "Okay?"

"Well, I think Aunt Vicki knows about you. I mean, she knows your name. I'm sure she won't tell anyone."

"No one," she stressed. "Especially not your family. You'll put me and them in danger. Please."

He frowned, not wanting to put anyone in danger, but not understanding how Aunt Vicki knowing would harm Nina. "Why?"

"Please. Just promise."

"All right, I won't," he assured her, placing his cap back on his head.

"Good. Don't forget the traps. Be ready," she reminded him.

"Okay." Jay fished the two items she'd given him out of his jeans pocket.

"There're three traps and you have everything you need to get through them." The door began closing, and right before the crack disappeared, she added, "Bye, Jay." And he was alone in the cold darkness again.

"Bye," he muttered with a lack of confidence. He reached into his other pocket for his flashlight and flicked it on, shining it down the rocky path. His face fell as he replayed her words in his head. "Wait. Three?"

He felt beads of sweat popping out of his skin, his body alternately burning with heat and then shivering with cold. "Three traps?" He swung around to face the door. "Nina!" he called out, "Nina! What do you mean three?" But she was long gone. She had to go to her Power Lesson, whatever that was, and she was late. She wouldn't be standing there, waiting for him to come bumbling in again. And if the alien creatures caught him, Lord only knew what would happen. But, sheesh! She could have at least let him know what the third trap was. Why would she say that and not explain? Maybe he had misunderstood her. That was possible—and frankly, his only hope.

Staying alert to his surroundings, he strode down the large tunnel. The first trap was the snake and would be coming up soon. He tucked the artichoke-looking fruit into the waistband of his jeans and lifted his flashlight with a shaky hand. In the other, he held the coin by its string. He heard nothing, not even a hiss, which he supposed was the idea. A trap wouldn't work so great if you could sense it a mile off.

As he approached the crisscrossed tunnel, he attempted to shine the light into the darkness to the right, but it wouldn't penetrate all the cracks and crevices. Maybe the thing was still in a trance. He contemplated this for a brief instant before its ugly head popped out of the shadows like a possessed Jack-in-the-box.

It began shaking its tail, creating a rattling sound so loud he thought his eardrums might explode from the echo. He heard a woman screaming without realizing until after the event that the scream had come from his very own throat. The yellow eyes of the snake stared at him with its elliptic black pupils moving just slightly, looking him over with sinister intent. It seemed he was staring into the face of Satan himself.

It sees me. Oh God, it sees me. Its teeth bore the thick,

clear poison of death. Only after it opened its frightening jaws, which at its elongated length were about as tall as Jay, did he remember the coin. He jerked his hand up high, holding the string, shining his flashlight upon it. The gold coin glistened, and the monster's large eyes fell upon it.

Abruptly, the creature froze. Its mouth snapped shut as it stared at the coin with greed. Jay rocked it back and forth, forth and back, three times, as Nina had instructed. On the third and final time, the snake bolted upright, taller than his house, and fell into a trance. Jay sighed and wiped his face, unaware he'd been crying. "Crazy!" he muttered. "Freakin' crazy!"

The creature almost completely blocked off the path. He squeezed past its body and the rock wall, grimacing at the cold, slippery texture of its skin as it brushed his own. Chills ran up and down him at its touch.

Jay continued on wobbly legs, like he hadn't eaten or slept for days. All his limbs seemed to have had their usefulness frightened out of them. With shaky hands, he maintained the grip on his flashlight and almost dropped the coin as he placed it back into his pocket. He fished out the flesh-colored fruit and prepared himself for the next trap, mentally and physically. As he moved on, he swore he wouldn't allow himself to be surprised again.

The crocodile was coming up ahead, and his heart burned with anticipation. The monster's den was as dark as the snake's had been, and again, there was no sign that anything dwelled there. He didn't want to wait for the thing to pop out at him, so instead, he threw the fruit into the shadows on his left where the beast had been before, then waited. Nothing happened. No hissing, no chomping—nothing.

Jay had no idea what to do. He wondered if he should just go on. Perhaps it was sleeping, and he could sneak by. How long was he to wait?

It turned out not long at all. He shifted his focus from the tunnel on the left to the one on his right to find two red eyes reflecting in the darkness. The crocodile wobbled into the light and turned its humongous, pointed snout in Jay's direction. Next came a horrifying sound, which reminded him of a car trying to start, except no car had ever sparked such fear in him as this did.

His heart fell into his stomach and seemed to catch on fire as he realized he had thrown the fruit on the wrong side. "Crap," he whispered and backed away as the monster hissed and approached him. He shifted his eyes to the left, looking for the fruit, afraid to take his full attention off his predator. He saw nothing but blackness, with no idea how far it had gone within that darkness, much less how he'd be able to retrieve it.

With Jay's focus averted, the beast seized the opportunity, charging at him and smashing into his arm with its snout. One of its razor-sharp teeth knocked the flashlight from his hands, and he fell back a few feet, landing on his side. His cap flew off, skittering somewhere behind him. The flashlight clinked as it rolled away, coming to a stop against the wall. Jay quickly maneuvered onto his butt to find the creature in front of him, illuminated in an eerie glow, making it appear unreal—like something in a haunted house. Its top tooth was about as long as his forearm. With no problem, it could have split him in two. *Apparently, this guy likes to play with his food*, he thought.

Jay couldn't have screamed if he wanted to. His body was stiff, like rigor mortis had set in. All he could do was watch as the crocodile's massive jaws, with their yellow, oversized sharp teeth, drew near.

At this, the end of his young life, he thought of his dad. He'd been through so much pain. It wasn't fair that he would have to go through all of that again. He wasn't sure Dad's heart could take it. "I'm sorry," Jay told him. "I'm so sorry."

15

WAR-TORN

Jay recalled watching a documentary about crocodiles on Animal Planet. When the crocodile wanted to eat something that was larger than one bite, it would clamp its jaws down on it and spin its own body around and around, ripping chunks off, shattering bones, and tearing off limbs. The "death roll," he remembered the show calling it. What a horrible, painful way to die. As he sat on his butt in the dark, defenseless and vulnerable, he supposed the death roll was to be his fate. As he watched the beast draw near, he almost wished the thing would get it over with and end his torture.

It's hot, rancid breath blew his hair, smelling like a mixture of death and terrible halitosis. He resisted the urge to close his eyes to prepare for his worst nightmare, instead focusing on the flashlight lying up against the tunnel wall a few feet away. Could he make a break for it? The beast seemed to take its sweet time, knowing full well it had the upper hand with no way out for its victim, enjoying every second of Jay's terror.

However, this monster wasn't aware of how strong Jay's determination was. He wasn't ready to die. Although he did not understand what it all entailed, he knew a lot of work remained for him in this life.

Jay tightened his lips and dove from his butt to his belly for the flashlight, his arms outstretched. His palms burned once again as they scraped the ground, but the pain was nothing compared to the persistence that raged inside him. The crocodile's jaws snapped together dangerously close as Jay snatched the flashlight in his fist. With bravery, he held the light up to the creature's eyes and it blinked, seeming to cringe. It had been in the darkness for so long, Jay supposed, it didn't seem to enjoy the sudden light shining into its eyeballs very much.

"How ya' like that?" he said with a vengeance as he took advantage of the reptile's temporary blindness and leapt to his feet. He darted to the right, but before he could escape, its massive tail swung at him, slamming into his legs and gut. The force knocked the wind out of him and hurled him to the back of the lair like a hockey puck.

Facing away from the creature, his eye caught the fruit lying ahead in the middle of the path. Jay scrambled for it, hearing the reptile's feet slap the rock floor as it came after him. Crocodiles are fast runners, he recalled, hoping and praying he would reach the fruit before he was seized by the beast's massive jaws. Jay was fast too, but was he fast enough?

He dove again, this time for the fruit, sliding on his chest and scooping it into his arms like a football. He twisted his body around and sat on the hard rock floor, his legs outstretched. With no time for triumph, he held the fruit up in one hand, shining his flashlight on it with the other just as the thing snapped at his right foot with its sharp teeth. Jay braced himself for the pain and even cried out before he felt anything. He clenched his eyes shut, not wanting to see all the blood, waiting for the sting to hit his brain.

When the pain never came, Jay opened his eyes and shined his light on his foot, revealing only a ripped sock with his toes sticking out and not a scratch on them. He looked up to see the beast standing still as stone, glaring at the enchanted fruit in Jay's outstretched hand as if it was a ball and he a dog waiting for its master to play catch with him. His shoe hung from the crocodile's open mouth, the laces dangling off one sharp tooth. On the verge of hyperventilation, he took a deep breath, having forgotten all about his need for oxygen for a moment.

He grinned with relief, but his smile faded when the beast began approaching him again. Jay knew he would have to rid himself of the object of this thing's desire or be tackled by its enormous mass. Yet, he would have to throw it far enough out of the way to remove its large body from blocking the exit. That was the trick.

With an opening targeted, he leaned left, still on his bottom. "You want it? You want this, you big, stupid, ugly jerk?" he asked, waving it. He threw the fruit hard over the creature's body where the two tunnels crossed. The beast followed with its eyes as far as possible before waddling out backwards, Jay's shoe swinging from side to side from its mouth. When it was able, it turned around and disappeared into the blackness of the adjacent tunnel, its huge tail tracing the ground back and forth with its tip, forgetting all about Jay sitting there—a fat piece of meat ready to be eaten. When it found the fruit, Jay heard the hissing and chomping noises just as he had when he passed the croc on the way to the Great Room. "I should've been on the football team," he mused.

But there was no time to celebrate. He scrambled into the main tunnel and took off toward the exit, more shaken than ever, the coldness of the floor biting through his half-torn sock.

He stopped in his tracks, remembering something.

Nina had mentioned the fruit would enchant the beast for about twenty minutes, so he knew he had some time. He circled back to where the crocodile attacked him and searched the ground with his flashlight until he found what he was looking for. As he snatched it up, the creature made the loud car starting sound, just about making Jay collapse where he stood. He yanked his cap back on and bolted for the exit, wondering to himself what he was thinking—going back for a baseball cap! But it was his favorite, and afterwards he thought it'd totally been worth it.

"Where are you?" he asked the cave walls as he slowed down, scanning them as he walked, hoping the exit with the X he'd drawn on the wall would show up soon. He desperately wanted out of the dark tunnels and into the daylight, breathing fresh air, and going back to living his life. And, yet...

"Three traps," Nina had said.

"Maybe she meant to say two. Oh, please let her have meant to say two," Jay whined. There'd only been two traps on the way there, after all. A third trap couldn't just turn up out of nowhere. Still, he searched up and around the cave walls with his light to be safe.

As he crept, examining the ceiling, something long and thin hit his ankle and made him tumble forward. His flashlight fell out of his hands as he braced himself. It remained lit and didn't roll very far, but his knees now ached to the point beyond what he could bear. He writhed in pain until the sting subsided, holding his legs close to his chest. As he reached to retrieve the flashlight, he spotted a very thin wire where he'd tripped, the size of a spider web, hardly noticeable.

"Really?" he asked, almost laughing, unimpressed. "That's the trap?" He breathed in deeply, the air feeling good in his lungs, bringing relief. No wonder Nina hadn't bothered to tell him about it. She might have saved him a couple of sore palms and kneecaps, but that's it. That meant less than nothing to him. The only thing that mattered was he was done. The hard part was over, and he would soon be out. What a great feeling it was, and he wished it would last forever.

Yet, it didn't even last one minute.

As he stood, he heard a rumbling noise growing louder and louder until it became a roar. A rush of wind hit him as the air seemed to vibrate with intensity. Something was coming, something massive, its presence looming, as though the very ground trembled beneath its power. He shot the beam of light toward the sound to discover its source. A body of darkness was approaching at a rapid speed. A wall of water!

"Oh, crap!" Jay ran as fast as his aching legs could carry him, hearing the water roar with fury behind as it coated his limbs with spray.

It was very close, maybe right on his heels for all he knew. He had no idea where the exit was or how far away he was from it. He would never make it! How was he going to make it?

If ever he needed a miracle, it was right then. He reached up to his neck to grab his mother's ring to ask for one, remembering with anguish that it was gone.

Yet he got one anyway. The black X appeared on the wall in front of him, and he dashed into it without a thought. Forgetting all about the two-foot drop, he leapt over it and almost lost his footing, his body going faster than his legs for a moment.

The wave hit the entrance to the rusty pipe with a loud bang, shaking the entire structure and making it seem too unstable to be in. As he ran, the water gushed into the pipe and struck his back and legs, pushing him forward. Once on the other side, the flood engulfed him. He would drown soon if he didn't hurry.

He reached for the first rung, but the water caused him to rise faster than he could climb, and he bypassed it along with all the other rungs as it carried him up like magic. He was thankful he hadn't been even two steps further back, or it would have trapped him inside the pipe for sure.

With his arm over his head to prevent bearing the brunt of the manhole cover, he shot up out of the ground like a cannon and landed on the grass, knocking the wind out of his lungs. His cap flew off as water rose like a geyser beside him.

When it was all over and the water had subsided, he rolled onto the wet, muddy grass, struggling to catch his breath. Exhausted, he coughed up the dirty liquid, its taste of metal and filth lingering in his mouth. With his clothes and skin torn, and one shoe missing, he must have resembled someone washed ashore after being lost at sea. He lay there for a long while before attempting to move, each shift of his body sending waves of pain through him.

Thankful for the bushes surrounding him, hopefully shielding him from view in his war-torn state, he grabbed his wet cap and plopped it on. His body was wracked with pain as he limped to the spot where Smith had yanked the necklace off him. He was soaked and tired, his sock black with filth, and every movement of his legs seemed to require more energy than he had in him. But he had to find it at all costs.

Sure enough, he spotted his mother's ring, right where Nina had said it would be, glistening in the setting sun. He clamped it in his fist and trudged home, wondering if after getting past the monster-sized snake, the enormous crocodile, and the near drowning with his body still intact, it would be fatigue that would kill him.

When he finally made it home, he collapsed onto his bed, unable to believe what had happened. The only proof of it was his wet, filthy, torn clothes, his bruised and broken skin, and a strange marking on his ankle—a symbol now smudged beyond recognition. He didn't think he'd ever been so grimy in his life, or so worn out in every way, emotionally, physically, and mentally.

The thought hit him: Nina had been watching him this whole time. He'd known something was off with that dog all along, he just hadn't figured out what. But these questions remained—why was this girl following him? Why him? And how could a place like Stoneburrow, where aliens lived alongside humans, exist? Was this real, or had it been only a dream? Had he passed out when he'd fallen on the concrete after Smith had tripped him? Perhaps he would wake up in a hospital bed any minute now. His head did hurt. A lot, actually. He rubbed his temples with the tips of his fingers, willing the scenario to be true.

Thankfully, he'd managed to sneak into the house undetected. Now, he'd have to clean himself up fast before Dad found him. But did he have the strength? That was the question.

16

NOT SAFE

Somehow, Jay managed to shower and change with what little energy he had remaining after such a weird and draining day. He hobbled out of the bathroom in a long-sleeved T-shirt—meant to hide the bruises— and jeans, clutching his soaked but freshly cleaned Colorado Rockies baseball cap.

He was taken aback to find Dad standing in the middle of his room, surrounded by Jay's dirty clothes and clutter, arms crossed and his face twisted like he'd bitten into something sour. "What the heck happened in here?" he spat, not a trace of compassion in his voice. If only he knew.

Jay tried his best to sound innocent. "What do you mean?"

"You're kidding, right?"

Jay sighed, unsure he had the strength to handle what was about to happen and hoping beyond hope that it all might disappear before his eyes. He had a pounding headache, and every joint and muscle in his body hurt. The only cure was sleep, but it would be a while before he could. Dad wasn't about to let this go quickly. He so wished he could pass the hypnotic coin he'd used on the snake in front of his dad's face a few times and put him into a trance—only for a couple days.

"Look at this place!" Dad motioned to the floor. "Where did you go? I thought you went to work with Vicki." Dad squinted as he approached Jay, who responded by backing up a bit. "What happened to your face?"

Jay reached up to his cheek. "Uh…"

"You're all scraped up. Did you get into another fight?" Dad stuck his finger out in accusation. "You did, didn't you?"

"No, Dad."

"Tell me the truth."

"I didn't. I swear!"

"Well, something must have happened." He motioned to the mess on the floor. "And you're going to tell me what, understand?"

"I *have* told you—"

"I don't want to hear lies. I'll have you know, while you were taking a relaxing shower, I was on my hands and knees, scrubbing up the nasty, muddy footprints you left all over this house." For someone who didn't care much about his own appearance, Dad sure liked to keep things clean. *So* weird. His glasses were always gross, and he rarely bathed, but he would scour the carpet if he suspected even a hint of a stain.

"Sorry." Jay kept his head down, focusing on the pile of soiled clothes at Dad's feet.

"Well, sorry doesn't take away the hassle. Tell me where you've been!"

"Just messing around. Nothing big. Got a little scraped up." He pulled down his sleeves as far as possible to hide his sore arm, thankful his jeans hid the giant bruise on his hip (which he only recently discovered while showering) and some various bruises on his legs. "Stupid stuff. It happens."

"Not with you, Jay. This is highly unusual." Dad pushed the smudgy glasses up the bridge of his nose with the knuckles of his right hand. "I mean, look at you. You look like you've been in some horrific accident. Obviously, you've been fighting again."

"I told you I haven't." This was in fact true. He hadn't fought anyone and the only wound he obtained from being bullied by Smith and Thad was the scrape on his cheek.

"Sorry, bud. I'm grounding you."

"What? That's not fair!"

"It's for your own good. You're grounded for a month."

"What? Why?"

"I have to keep you safe from this Brian kid. He's dangerous. If you stay in for a month, maybe this whole thing will blow over." Dad waved his hands, perhaps hoping to erase it all.

"Not cool! This has nothing to do with Brian." He hadn't even seen him that day. But nothing he could have said would have been good enough to change Dad's mind. Especially not the truth. "I can still go to the Humane Society, right?"

"No, you may not. You're grounded, Son."

"But, why?" Jay whined. "I told you I wasn't fighting. Why don't you believe me?"

"You have wounds all over you. That's why!" He reached over and yanked up Jay's shirt sleeve to reveal a long, jagged cut. "You don't think I saw this? For God's sake!" He inspected closer, grimacing. "Looks like you've been through World War Three!"

"But—"

Dad held up his hand. "I know you would say almost anything to go to the Humane Society and I appreciate that. But this is what's best for now. You're not safe out there. You just aren't."

"That's so unfair!" Dad was acting insane, but that was just how he always was. Jay couldn't take another second of it. With no escape, he stormed back into the bathroom and slammed the door shut, locking it behind him.

Dad began pounding on it, screaming at him from the other side. "Jay, open the door." Although Dad was persistent, Jay ignored it. "I can't lose you too!"

Jay flicked on the fan and sat on the edge of the toilet seat, pressing his hands over his ears until Dad's voice faded into nothing but a faint buzz.

17

TEARS AND RAIN

Thirty days was a long time to keep a secret like Nina and the underground world to himself. Jay thought a lot about his adventure during his sentence. As the weeks passed, his wounds healed and disappeared, but his desire to learn more about Stoneburrow remained.

Sometimes, when he daydreamed about his adventures underground, he wondered if it had all just been a dream, or maybe a movie he'd seen and somehow had mistaken for real life. It seemed too unbelievable. Images of the dark tunnels and the vast Great Room replayed in his mind on a loop. Remembering the crocodile, the snake, and the wall of water still made his heart race. He could barely focus on anything else.

And then there was Nina. A girl that could turn herself into a dog. It was mind boggling.

"I found out your secret, Aunt Vicki," he whispered as he sat at his desk, drawing Nina in her dog form in his sketching pad. Aunt Vicki had been hiding what she knew about Nina. But how much of it did she actually know? Surely, she knew Nina was a human. Was she also aware aliens lived underground with her? He wanted to ask, but he couldn't. He wouldn't break his promise to Nina. At least not now. He wasn't sure about forever.

On Sunday, the last day of his grounding, Jay helped Aunt Vicki finish preparing a pot roast that had been cooking for hours, filling up the room with a fragrance of meat, onions, and potatoes you could almost taste in the air.

Jay didn't understand how Aunt Vicki could resist eating the delicious food she prepared. So weird that she was okay with cooking animals, but not eating them. When Jay had asked her about it before, she'd said, "Someone has to cook it. Might as well be me." Neither Dad nor Jay would eat her beans and sprouts. She'd learned that from experience, but it wasn't from a lack of trying on her part. She knew they would live off Frosted Flakes and Fruity Pebbles until they passed out from constipation if she didn't cook the meat Dad was insistent on eating.

"How're the animals?" Jay asked her as he mashed the potatoes and she stirred the gravy. Dad loved mashed potatoes with pot roast, and Aunt Vicki always made what Dad liked. She'd made his favorites for most every meal since moving into the guesthouse years ago.

"Just fine," she told him, glancing at him sideways with a smile. "You'll know tomorrow when you come in, I suppose."

"I know. I can't freakin' wait." His heart lifted at the thought that his grounding was almost over. It felt almost too good to be true.

Aunt Vicki laughed softly. "Well, we've missed you, that's for sure."

"Thanks, Aunt Vicki. I have too." However, he wasn't even close to being as excited to see his dog and cat friends as he was to see Nina. He had so many questions to ask her.

Dad marched in, swinging open the refrigerator, making the various bottles inside the door rattle. "Food smells great."

"It's almost done," Aunt Vicki said. "Go ahead and have a seat. Can you get the plates, Jay?"

Jay obeyed, eager to be on his best behavior. As they all sat down to eat, it seemed this was a celebratory meal. And Jay totally felt like celebrating. Just one more day and he would be free.

"Tomorrow's the day, huh?" Dad asked him as he unfolded a napkin into his lap, seeming to read his mind.

"Yup."

Dad started digging into the platter of food, piling his dish high with steaming meat and vegetables. "What's tomorrow look like for you?"

"After my schoolwork, I'll go to the Humane Society, as always."

Dad made a subtle face. "Are you sure that's a good idea? Pass me your plate, Jay."

"Sure, why not?" he asked as he obeyed.

"We don't need another Brian incident." Dad heaped meat on Jay's plate. "God help me, I hate that kid. You want mashed potatoes too?"

Jay nodded and reached out to accept his dish. "I can get it myself."

"Gene," Aunt Vicki interjected. "You don't *hate* anybody."

He huffed. "You'd be surprised." He turned back to Jay as he plopped a spoonful of potatoes next to the helping of pot roast, ignoring his request. Shoving the plate toward him, he softened his expression once more. "I really don't think you should go."

Jay shrugged. "It'll be fine. It always is."

Dad huffed. "Not always."

"Most always."

"It only takes one time for something to happen and for you to get hurt badly. It only takes a moment to..." Dad's eyes shifted away. "To destroy a person."

"Yeah, but—"

Dad interrupted. "I don't feel good about you walking alone."

"Dad," Jay whined.

"As I've said, I don't think it's a good idea." He adjusted his glasses, looking irritated.

"Then can I ride my bike?"

"That's not the point. I don't want you to go alone."

"Then what? Are *you* gonna go with me?"

"Um." Dad's focus went to his untouched food, his lips in a tight line, his brow narrowed.

"Of course not. You won't because you never leave the house!" Jay spouted, anger bubbling inside him.

Aunt Vicki gasped, but Dad ignored her. "Jay, it's not that I don't want to leave the house. I...I just get busy."

"Busy doing what? You don't do anything! In the morning, you trade stocks on the computer and that's it. On the weekends, all you do is watch movies and mess around on the internet."

Dad pointed a piece of meat he'd stabbed with his fork at Jay. "Now that's not true. I have to research companies. I have to decide my strategies."

"Bull," Jay mumbled, realizing he wasn't the least bit hungry.

"Jay, let it go. It'll be okay," Aunt Vicki told him in a soothing voice.

But Jay would have nothing of it. "No, it won't! If you won't let me walk or ride my bike there, how am I supposed to go to the Humane Society?" When he didn't answer right away Jay asked again, desperate for an answer. "How, Dad?"

"Maybe Vicki could come get you?" Dad peered at Aunt Vicki followed by Jay doing the same, watching her expression change from concern to confusion, then uncertainty.

"Now, Gene," she reasoned. "That's not realistic. I can't just leave. I mean, there may be times when I can, but for the most part, I wouldn't be able to do that."

"Great!" Jay threw his fork down onto the plate and a sharp ring filled the air as mashed potatoes splatted across the table. "That's great. I've been looking forward to going for a month and now you won't let me? This sucks!" He jumped up, almost knocking over his chair as it squealed across the floor.

"What are you doing? Where are you going?" Dad raised a hand. "We need to talk about it, Jay."

"Talk about what? There's no talking to you."

"Sit back down."

Jay's face flushed with anger. "I am not Mom."

"What?" Dad frowned, his voice softening. "No. I know."

"I'm not going to die!" Jay clenched his fists at his sides. "I want to go live my life! Why won't you let me?"

"Jay, you'll understand when you're older."

"No! I won't. I'll never understand you! And I am not a little kid, so stop talking to me like that!"

Dad tightened his mouth, food tucked inside his cheek. "Come on. Sit down."

"I'm done. I'm going to my room." Jay had had enough, his appetite now nonexistent.

"Oh, no you're not," Dad commanded. "Vicki took time to cook this delicious meal, and you will eat it. Sit your butt right back down or I'll ground you for a couple more days."

"That's crap! I'm grounded for not eating now? You're just looking for a reason to keep me grounded longer. You're such a jerk!" Moisture blurred Jay's vision as he tried desperately to hold it in. The back of his throat burned like fire.

"That's it. You've forced my hand. Two more days."

"What? You've got to be kidding me! Aunt Vicki?"

Aunt Vicki shook her head, shrugging her shoulders and lowering her gaze to her plate.

Jay turned back at his dad, scowling. Dad was acting like a bully—just as much as Brian was. He couldn't go anywhere to get away from them.

Dad exhaled. "I understand you love being with the animals, Jay, and it kills me to have to do this. It's for your own good."

"It doesn't kill you! This is what you want. And you don't know what's good for me! You have no idea!"

"Jay, I—"

"What does it matter? You might as well ground me

for life! You want to keep me locked in this house like you are, afraid of the world. I'm not afraid of the world! If I get beat up trying to live in it, then I do. So, what! At least I'm trying. Unlike you!" Jay took off sprinting up the stairs to his room.

"Jay, wait," Dad called out to him. "You don't understand."

"I understand," Jay mumbled to himself as he reached the top of the staircase. "I totally understand." He slammed his door behind him, his emotions spent, and plopped down at his desk to peer out the window.

It was overcast and rainy as thunder roared, mirroring the roar of anger inside his chest. Jay watched the rain pouring down in sheets, tears running down his cheeks, mimicking it. He opened the window wide, listening to the downpour of water hit the house as light spray coated his face, mixing with his tears. In silence, he watched the storm's tyrannical effects to the lawn, and he wondered when this would stop. When would the rain stop beating down on his life? When would he feel the sun beating on him instead? Would there ever be relief?

More importantly, would he ever see Nina again? Perhaps she had forgotten him by now. He'd told her before he got grounded that he would see her soon. Soon had come and gone a long time ago—a month to be exact. She probably thought he was avoiding her on purpose. Maybe after all that had happened underneath the earth, she thought he was afraid. And now here he was, grounded again, even before he could become ungrounded.

"This blows," he told his goldfish, Samson, who observed him through the water bowl with no sympathy.

"I can't wait until I'm eighteen." But that wouldn't be for another two plus years, and he needed to be free now.

He pulled the gold coin from his pants pocket where he had been keeping it since the day Nina had given it to him, the string still tied through the hole. As he rubbed it with his thumb, an image of her filled his brain—sitting in the usual spot in her dog form, drenched in rain, waiting. He covered his face with both hands to block it all out.

18

WE'VE ALWAYS BEEN

Dad stepped into Jay's room the next day after lunch, finding him lying face down on the bed with his history book open in front of him. "Hello," he said in a low voice. This time, he was in his gray sweats with a blue T-shirt that Jay was pretty sure he'd worn for the last three days straight.

After glancing at his chest briefly, refusing to give him the benefit of eye contact, Jay returned his chin to his fists and pretended to read. Through his peripheral vision, he noticed Dad's hands on his hips. Although the visor of Jay's cap hid Dad's face, Jay imagined he was frowning. "I talked to Vicki this morning. She believes I was too hard on you."

Jay ignored him, thinking about how perceptive Aunt Vicki could be.

"She might be right. Maybe I'm a little strict." This was met with more silence as Jay wrestled with himself to keep from blurting out, *Duh!* "I worry about you, Jay," Dad whined. "I'm overprotective. Shoot me." His palms slapped to his sides in frustration and after a deep sigh, he continued, "Vicki seems to think you'll be okay going to the Humane Society today." Upon hearing this, Jay lifted the bill of his cap and peered up to him with his eyes only. "I'm letting you go," Dad said, in a lackadaisical tone.

"You are?" He was almost afraid to believe it.

"Yes." Dad put both hands up as a barrier. "But I'm not happy about it."

Jay shot up onto his knees. "Thank you, Dad! Thank you! When can I go?"

Dad sighed, clearly not enjoying his son's enthusiasm. After a few seconds of agonizing silence, he spoke, "Tell you what, you finish up that chapter and you can leave."

"For real?"

Dad nodded, closing and opening his eyes slowly, unwilling to say it again.

"Sweet. Thanks!"

Dad tilted his head, fixing Jay with a serious look. "But that Brian kid bugs you again, I want you to tell me. Is that a deal?"

"Yeah, whatever. Yeah." *Sure, so you can ground me again?* Jay wasn't stupid. But for now, he would agree to whatever was necessary to get out of that house. The most important thing was finding Nina. That's all he cared about.

"Take your bike."

"Really? Thanks, Dad."

"Son, you thanked me enough." Dad managed a faint smile before stepping into the hallway and pulling the door shut behind him.

Jay skimmed through the chapter, comprehending

very little. After about ten minutes, he hurried down the stairs to find Dad in his den. Jay straightened his cap, framing the bill before announcing, "I'm leaving," poking his head inside.

"Already?"

"Yup."

"Any questions about the history chapter?"

"Nope." Jay shifted his weight from foot to foot, waiting for the word so he could bolt.

"Did you finish the questions at the end?"

Oh, crap. "Um."

"I'll take that as a no."

"Come on." Going back upstairs and sitting in front of that history book would be a fate worse than death.

Dad chuckled. "All right. As long as you do those in the morning."

"Awesome."

Jay raced out the door, grabbed his bike, and rode as fast as his legs would allow all the way to Nina's spot. The sidewalks and street were dry now, no puddles to be found. Even the smell of rain was gone from the air, leaving instead the aroma of flowers and weeds baking in the sun.

As Jay approached Nina's usual spot, he noticed the dog's black paws poking out from behind a bush. "Nina!" he called out, jumping off his bike and letting it fall to the ground. The dog popped its head around the shrub in a rather unnatural way, then ducked back, her large ears flopping with each movement. "Nina?" When he rounded the bushes, she was gone. "Nina? Where are you?" He pulled the cover aside and peered into the darkness. "Nina?" His voice echoed as he aimed his flashlight down the hole, the beam catching only the wet floor glinting far below. "I'm sorry," he said quietly. "It wasn't my fault."

After a few moments, he replaced the cover with disappointment. He remembered the snake, the crocodile and the rush of water that had threatened to drown him. "No way I'm going down there," he muttered to himself. "I won't." Frustrated, he planted his butt on the grass. He didn't mean to stay away so long. Surely, she would understand if she'd only let him explain.

The lid popped open almost five minutes later and a girl's face appeared, startling him. She seemed tired, out of breath, and sweaty. "Hi." She pulled her small body up from the pipe with her two pale, skinny arms.

"Hey." Jay beamed with relief. "I thought you ghosted me."

Nina parroted his grin while plopping down next to him, crisscrossing her legs as she caught her breath, wiping her wet, blonde hair off her moist face. She wore the same oversized peach-colored shirt she'd had on the last time he saw her. With it, this time, she sported black, tight-fitting pants, the bottoms wet and her feet bare. "That's funny. You actually thought I was a ghost?"

"No." Jay said with a soft laugh, shaking his head. "I thought you were done with me."

She wrinkled her nose. "Done?"

"Like ignoring me, you know."

"Oh." She allowed it all to sink in for a moment. "No, I had to leave the collar down in the hole."

"Your collar? Why?"

"It's enchanted to change me into a dog in this atmosphere. If I go down, it changes me back. I can't very well take it off with no thumbs," she told him, wiggling them.

The two sat in silence for a moment. "That's really weird."

"Yeah."

"Can I try it?"

"Try what?" Nina squinted, scrunching her nose again.

"Can I change into a dog?"

"Oh, no." Her eyes widened. "It's enchanted for me. Might be dangerous."

Jay nodded, thinking perhaps she was lying. She wouldn't meet his eyes for more than a fraction of a second before glancing away again, which seemed to support that theory. Though, he didn't care so much about that. He had so many other questions that had been running through his brain all month that he didn't know quite where to begin. "Oh, almost forgot. Here's your coin." He fished it out of his pocket and passed it to her.

Her eyes brightened. "Thanks! I've been spraying stuff in the snake's eyes to get around it."

"What?"

"Yeah. The coin is so much easier. Without it, I have to spray something into its eye and run like crazy."

"Yikes."

She peered beyond Jay's head, fear in her eyes as if remembering. "It's scary."

"I guess so. Sorry."

"You were gone a long time." She seemed to snap out of it and dropped the coin into her pocket.

"I know. I didn't mean to be. My stupid dad grounded me for a month."

"Grounded?"

"My dad is strict and grounds me a lot. It's lame."

Nina frowned.

Her expression made Jay chuckle. "You don't know what *grounded* means."

She shook her head, keeping the scowl in place.

At first, he thought Nina might be a ditz, but he realized she just didn't know what a lot of words meant. It was weird to imagine this girl living underground with no idea what went on above it, let alone how kids her age talked. He might have to explain a lot of things to her, and he was okay with that. "It means he won't let me leave the house for a certain amount of time. It's a punishment."

Her face softened with understanding. "Why did he ground you? What did you do wrong?"

"He thought I got my face beat in." When she frowned at him again, he rolled his eyes. "I know. Stupid, right?" Jay shook his head. "I wasn't even fighting. That's what really ticks me off. This dude tripped me, and I faceplanted on the concrete. With that, and after all the freakin' bruises I got from following you underground, Dad just assumed I'd gotten into a fight."

"Why do those boys hate you so much?" Nina looked sympathetic. She might have even pitied him. He didn't like that.

"They screw with a lot of people, not just me. I guess it makes them feel powerful. Especially Brian."

"Oh."

Jay chuckled. "When you attacked him? That was

epic!" He held one hand to his stomach that was already starting to cramp. "I should have known you weren't actually a dog when you jumped on his back."

"Why? Dogs don't jump on people's backs?"

"Uh, no. Not usually."

They laughed together. "I didn't know how else to stop him," she said.

"Well, it worked." Jay's smile lingered, even after their laughter died down.

Nina finally broke the silence. "How old are you, Jay?"

"I'm fifteen. How old are you?"

"I'm about twelve or so."

"About?"

Nina pursed her lips, focusing on something in the distance. "I don't know exactly when I was born."

"Wow. That's weird."

"Not really. In Stoneburrow, we don't celebrate birthdays like outsiders do. We don't find the date to be awfully important."

Jay raised his brow. "It's like a huge deal for us." How could you live without knowing your birthday?

"Yeah." Nina muttered, chewing on the corner of her bottom lip. Her eyes flicked away like she wasn't interested in talking about it anymore.

"Why were you following me?" This was something he wanted to ask her since he'd been to her underground world, and he just kind of blurted it out, eager to know.

Nina examined her grimy fingernails, saying nothing. Her long hair fell onto one shoulder. "I can't tell you." The dirt didn't deter her from biting her nails with anxiousness.

"Why not?"

"I can't. I will. Just not right now."

"I don't get it. Why the secret?"

She shrugged her shoulders, her fingers still in her mouth. "Just can't."

"Fine. Can I ask you something else then?"

"Okay," Nina answered with uncertainty as she continued to gnaw on her nails, now from the side, studying him with curiosity.

"What are you?"

She dropped her hands into her lap and glared at him like he'd insulted her although that wasn't his intention. "What kind of question is that?"

"Sorry. I meant, where are you from? Like, what planet?"

"Planet?"

"You know what I mean." Jay sighed, rubbing the back of his neck. "Where are your people from? Like, those freaky creatures. Where'd they come from?"

"The Grays?" she said, like he should know the word.

"I guess. Yeah, whatever. Those guys."

"The Grays are from here, as I am. As we all are." She spoke with confidence, clearly believing what she was saying, although it made no sense.

"From here?"

"Yes. We are two different races, Units and Grays. Like you have different races of people on the outside. We're from here like you, only we're from under the earth's surface and you're from above it," she explained, as if it was all really quite simple.

"How long have you been down there?"

"We've always been here, Jay." She flashed him a small smile. "We've always been."

"Jay?" a voice called from the other side of the bush.

"Lydia!" Jay uttered under his breath, jumping to his feet and scrambling out of the bushes. Lydia appeared like a vision—beautiful in her light blue tank top and blue jean shorts, her long black hair tied up into a ponytail. When he saw her, along with the familiar feelings of fascination and awe, he also felt an unfamiliar twinge of anger. "Lydia, hi."

"What are you doing, Jay? Who are you talking to?"

He shook his head, his voice coming out a higher pitch than he'd intended. "What do you mean? No one." His eyes darted left, briefly focusing on the bush in his peripheral, silently hoping Nina had hidden herself.

When he returned his gaze to Lydia, she'd narrowed her painted eyebrows into a frown. She could do with a little less makeup. Her natural beauty was more than enough, and the eye stuff she wore was a bit much. "Nice try. I was in my house, and I heard you scream something. Then I came outside and you're talking away with someone in the bushes. Who is it?"

"Don't take this the wrong way, Lydia, but what do you care?" It felt like she was grilling him as if he'd done something wrong, and he wasn't a fan.

She reacted as if he'd slapped her. "Dang, Jay. I was just wondering." She squinted. "Why're you being such a jerk?"

Brian's words echoed in his mind as he studied her stunning, yet contorted face. *She totally played you, moron!* "I guess getting beat up a few times will do that to a person."

Lydia's expression resembled guilt but faded as

quickly as it had come, followed by a roll of her eyes and a sigh. "Sorry about that."

"You said that last time."

Lydia didn't react verbally but replied with a look conveying something. But what? *I'm sorry... I'm not sorry... I was wrong... Get over it.* He couldn't tell for sure.

"What are you doing here, anyway? I mean, in the middle of the day?" he asked her.

"Not sure how you, *homeschoolers* do it, Jay, but we lowly public school kids get summer vacations."

"Oh, right." It was summer break already? That was hard to believe. Jay had almost forgotten all about it because Dad wasn't about to give him one.

He glanced around her house, concerned that she might not be alone.

"You don't have to worry about Brian," she said. "I'm pissed at him. He's not here."

Jay fought back the grin that wanted to reveal itself and hoped this meant an end to their relationship. It would serve them both right.

"I still want to know who you were talking to. Is it your girlfriend?" Lydia took a step toward the bushes, only for Jay to block her path.

"No. I told you. There's no one." Was it his imagination, or was she acting jealous? Was that even possible? She sent him so many mixed signals it was pathetic.

Lydia placed her manicured hands on her small hips. "Does 'no one' have blonde hair?"

"What?"

"I can see blonde hair." She pointed to the bushes, making her way toward them again.

"It's nothing. It's dandelions or something. For real,

Lydia." Jay's palms were sweating, and his body temperature shot up. How would he explain a blonde twelve-year-old girl behind the bushes? This would not be good.

Lydia rounded the bushes with Jay on her tail. She stopped, and he caught up with her. Nina was gone. Jay resisted the urge to blurt out, "Whew!" and wipe the sweat off his forehead in an exaggerated motion. Instead, he shrugged and said, "See, I told you."

"I must be losing it." Lydia marched back to her house, her flip-flops slapping the pavement with each angry step. "I don't get why he's behind the freakin' bushes anyway, talking to himself," she mumbled to herself ironically. "He's legit insane!" Listening to her ramble as she stomped away made him smile for some reason.

Jay waited for Nina by the cover for about twenty minutes after Lydia left him before finally giving up and heading toward the Humane Society. Along the way, Nina's words replayed in his brain over and over. He couldn't get them out of his mind. "We've always been here, Jay. We've always been."

19

WELL-LOVED

He had the dream again, for the third time this month. This one was even more vivid and unsettling. Not speaking of it for so long had almost caused him to forget, but his subconscious was not allowing it.

The moon shone brightly, yet the only light he focused on came from a spot shining in the distance. The trees beckoned him forward, luring him to it. This time, he was alone from the start, and this time, he knew exactly what would happen.

Charred and burned, the house called out to him. Out of the rubble, the woman's head appeared, her hair white as snow and her blue eyes glowing bright, making her shine like a beacon—like an angel. Aspects of her face were blurry, but her eyes focused onto his, very much aware of his existence, smiling as if they shared a secret.

Then it happened. The demons, or whatever they were, grabbed her, engulfing her in red light. Her facial expression didn't change as she went down. She showed no panic, no fear, as they dragged her away. The glow disappeared, leaving darkness and emptiness in its place.

He awoke covered in sweat, struggling to throw off the covers that seemed to be lined with lead, and dropped his bare feet onto the rug. Through his window, the sunrise glowed bright with color as cool air refreshed him from the vent along the wall below.

Not only were those demon things spine-chilling, but something about them was also familiar. "Can't think about it," he told himself, rubbing his face aggressively like he was trying to rub it off. He considered lying back down but knew he would never get back to sleep. After the dream he'd just had, he wasn't sure he wanted to, anyway.

He hauled himself into the kitchen, grabbed a bowl, and poured some Fruity Pebbles, his favorite. The chewing echoed inside his head, and he wished he could somehow shut it off, or at least turn it down a notch. "I should have helped her," he whispered. Why hadn't he? Why had he stood there like a lump—a wimpy loser doing nothing at all? But he couldn't fight demons. It wasn't like he was Superman or anything. So, it couldn't be his fault, right? Even so, it seemed he should have done something. "Not going to think about it," he reminded himself. Truthfully, he wasn't sure his memories of that night were even real. "Ghosts and demons?" It couldn't have been, could it?

After he got dressed and binge-watched a bunch of random videos for a couple of hours, he heard Aunt Vicki unlocking the back door and stepping into the kitchen. Immediately, she began making a lot of unnecessary noise, slamming cabinet doors and clinking dishes. "Hey, Jay. I'm making French toast. Want some?"

"Definitely, thanks." It had been two hours since he'd eaten, and his stomach rumbled again. French toast sounded amazing. "Need some help?"

"Love some." He plopped on a stool at the kitchen bar while Aunt Vicki dug all the ingredients they needed out of the pantry and refrigerator to make a meal she would never eat. "Where's your dad?" she asked.

"Um. I think he ran off and joined the circus or something."

"Ahh. Didn't have too far to go now, did he?" She popped her head out of the fridge before closing it, giving him a sly smile that made him laugh. "I guess we can let him sleep in today. The smell of food will wake him up soon enough."

Aunt Vicki always cooked breakfast for them on Saturday mornings. Jay loved that about her. "How's Ducky?" he asked.

"Just fine, thanks for asking," she sang. "Finally found someone to adopt the little guy."

"Oh, that's great."

"A very nice single mom with two young girls. He'll get lots of love."

A smile took over his face at the thought of Ducky being in a happy home. "What time are you going in today?"

"Not till lunchtime or so. Want to come with me?"

"Naw. Not today."

"Really?" Aunt Vicki closed a drawer a little rougher than she probably meant to, causing the silverware inside to clink. "Now that's surprising. I assumed you'd be itching to get out of here."

"I am," he told her as she set a bowl down in front of him alongside a carton of eggs. "How many?"

"Let's start with four. What are your plans?"

"I'll just hang out around the yard."

"By yourself?" The look she gave him held a bit of distrust, perhaps wondering what he was up to.

"Yeah." It wasn't exactly true. He was dying to see Nina again. He hadn't even begun to scratch the surface of all the questions he wanted to ask her.

"Why don't you try hanging out with Ishmael?"

Jay froze in mid-crack, his thumbs still inside the shell of the egg. "Aunt Vicki, would you lay off the Ishmael thing?" He felt if she mentioned his name even one more time, he might lose it. "I mean, come on."

"Okay, okay. I just worry about you being by yourself all day."

Sometimes he thought he'd be much better off if people would stop worrying about him. "It's not a big deal." He smeared egg juice onto the seat of his jeans, prompting a disapproving look from Aunt Vicki.

"Don't do that, Jay."

"Sorry," He turned away and rolled his eyes, grabbing a towel. "Maybe I'll go to the library." He'd been meaning to do that, anyway. There was something he needed to research.

"The library? On a Saturday? That's new." Aunt Vicki wore a strange air of longing on her face as she opened the milk, a telltale sign she was reminiscing. "Your mom used to take you to the library a lot."

"Yeah?"

Aunt Vicki smiled without revealing her teeth. "You loved to go. She read lots of books to you. You were so little then." She elbowed him in the arm. "I can't believe you'll be sixteen."

"Well, not for almost two months."

"I wish your mom was here to see how big you're getting."

"And what a geek I've become."

She smacked him lightly on the shoulder with the back of her hand. "Stop it. That's not true. Unless geek means smart, of course. Then yes, one hundred percent." He rolled his eyes again, this time with more exaggeration. "I remember the day you were born." She rested her chin on her knuckles, her elbows on the kitchen counter.

"You were there?" Jay said, and after about a quarter of a second, they both laughed in unison. This was funny because Aunt Vicki had told this story many times and he knew what was coming. He didn't mind though. He kind of loved it, actually.

"You were so tiny. So, so cute. Your mom and dad had such a hard time naming you. They couldn't agree on anything. After a while they gave up and decided to use the first name they heard when they got home and turned on the TV."

"Thank God Frankenstein wasn't on, or I'd be Igor right now."

Aunt Vicki cackled, deep and hearty. He loved it when something he said caused her to crack up like that. "Well, as you know, that never happened."

"I had to be in intensive care."

"Yep. The umbilical cord was wrapped around your neck, and you came out blue. They had to monitor you for a while to make sure everything was okay. Your parents were so worried, they kind of forgot about the television thing. It was a silly idea, anyway."

"Yeah, but they were kinda like that. So, you've told me."

"They sure liked to fly by the seat of their pants." She shook her head, remembering. "I knew that immediately after they eloped four weeks after they met." The way she talked, it was like both of Jay's parents had died and not just his mother. In some ways, Jay supposed they had. "Anyway, after the news about you having to spend the night in intensive care, your mom was so worried. As she was studying every inch of you, you peeped."

"Peeped or pooped?"

"Jay! You peeped—like a bird. I suppose, if you'd been a girl, your name would be Birdy or something."

Jay curled his lip. "Birdy?"

She snickered. "Or *something*. But instead—"

"They named me Jay."

"When you cried, you sounded like a baby bird. She used to call you her little birdy or jaybird."

"I remember."

"Up until the day she left us." They both grew quiet and solemn. "I sure miss her," she said with a crack in her voice, staring at the wall behind him. "She saved my life."

Jay had heard her say this many times but knew better than to ask about it. Any time he had, all she would tell him was his mother had saved Aunt Vicki's life when they were both kids. "She helped me get away from some bad people," was about as detailed as she got, never elaborating no matter how many questions he'd asked. He always wondered why she kept this such a secret.

And she seemed to be keeping an even bigger secret. She knew something about Nina, although it wasn't clear what. It was even possible she was aware of those alien, Gray things. Not being able to ask her was torture.

He supposed she had good reason for her hesitance to tell him things. When he was almost five years old, Jay remembered running into the house, yelling for his father in blood-curdling screams. He'd come from Aunt Vicki's guesthouse after barging in unannounced, although he was told to always knock. Sometimes he forgot about those small details.

Aunt Vicki was dead, he'd screamed. Dad had totally lost it and barreled over to Aunt Vicki's. He burst through the door while she, oblivious to Jay's harrowing episode, was wrapped in a towel, trying to find something to wear. This left all three of them red-faced—Aunt Vicki from embarrassment, Dad from anger, and Jay from fear.

He remembered a lot about that day. He'd really believed he had seen what he thought he'd seen. And to this day the picture remained crystal clear in his mind— her body laid out on the carpet in front of her bathroom, all her blood seemingly sucked out of her.

Aunt Vicki had calmed Dad down, telling him the trauma of his mother's death had caused Jay's breakdown. They'd gotten him a therapist, which he visited for almost a year. He remembered the doctor, a very nice and patient lady, had told them Jay was afraid of those he loved dying. Since Aunt Vicki had taken over the mother role, he especially worried for her, she'd said. That made sense to them all, even to Jay. So why were the images in his head still so clear and the horrible feeling so strong?

Why did he still wake up screaming sometimes after seeing it in his dreams?

Ever since that day, both Aunt Vicki and Dad had tried to protect him from everything. But he was a little kid, and his mom had just died, for crying out loud. Surely, they understood he'd grown a thicker layer of skin since then.

"Tara was so kind," Aunt Vicki continued, taking away his thoughts and bringing him back to the present. "She had the sweetest, softest heart of anyone I know."

"Or ever will," he said before she could.

"Dang, how I envied her eyelashes," she blurted as Jay laughed at her expression. "I never had good eyelashes."

He could honestly say he'd never noticed Aunt Vicki's eyelashes, or lack thereof. He couldn't say he'd ever noticed anyone's eyelashes, for that matter.

"For real, Jay! Everyone assumed they were fake. I swear they were real. She had a lovely oval face. I always wanted to look like her." She studied Jay with pools of water in her eyes. "You look like her."

"Oh, so I look like a pretty mom with lovely eyelashes?" he mocked in a feminine voice.

She laughed. The sharp jerk of her body caused the tears to break free and roll down both cheeks. "Dang it, Jay." She popped upright and wiped her face. "Now you've gone and made me cry."

"You always cry, Aunt Vicki."

"This is true. Shoot me for being emotional."

He placed his hand on Aunt Vicki's shoulder. "Aunt Vicki." His tone was soft as she smiled at him. "You know we don't keep guns in the house."

She shooed him off her, laughing again. "You brat! Help me with this food before your dad wakes up."

He snickered through his nose and began beating the eggs with a fork. "You crack me up, Aunt Vicki."

"And pass me the flippin' tissues. Good gosh!" He handed her the box with amusement as she pulled one out to dab her eyes. "Okay, that's enough water works." She sniffed as she retrieved the frying pan hanging over the kitchen bar.

"Aunt Vicki?" Jay's smile faded, causing hers to soften as well. "Why is Dad so sad all the time? Why does he still miss Mom so much?"

She released the air from her lungs through her nose and bowed her head, staring at the countertop. "He loved her. It was a true love so rare. It almost never happens."

"Is that why he never leaves the house? Why he gave up being a doctor?"

Her eyes filled with tears again as they met Jay's. "Yes, honey." She blew a waft of air from puckered lips. "That's why."

"I wish we could help him." Jay stirred the mixture, his heart heavy. There wasn't anything he wouldn't do to take away Dad's desolation, but that seemed impossible. "I wish Mom was still here."

"Me too." She took one more cleansing breath. "I said I wouldn't cry anymore. Let's get this meal done, shall we?"

Jay forced a smile. "Sorry."

"Hurry up with those eggs. Don't forget the cinnamon."

"I won't." Jay didn't know much, and these days he

wasn't positive of anything it seemed, but one thing he did knew for certain—Mom had been well-loved. Probably as much as anyone could be.

20

ISHMAEL

After breakfast, Jay headed outside, telling his dad he was going to hang out in the backyard for a while and read a book or just get some color to his albino skin. That didn't seem too promising since Dad made him wear SPF 60 before subjecting himself to sunshine (thus the albino skin) but it sounded good at least. With a couple of hours to spare before Dad would predictably scream his name from the door, he made his getaway down the street toward Nina's spot.

"Where are you, Nina?" He settled beside the cover, waiting, rising now and then to pace in restless circles. Occasionally, he opened it and peered down, but still, nothing. Disheartened, he gave up after about thirty minutes of restless agony and headed for the library. Maybe he would actually read like Dad thought he was doing.

The library was just a short walk away. Once inside, he headed to the computer section and searched the word "alien" in the library catalog under nonfiction. After some digging, he discovered a few books that looked promising.

Alien Abduction by Karl Huffman
The Alien Probes by Tan and Kim Lang
True Stories of Alien Encounters by Dr. Ralph Peterson

All of them were available. "Of course," he said to himself. "Who would read this stuff?" Heading to the shelves, he ran his finger along the spines, quickly locating all three. He tossed the books onto an empty table and took a seat, picking up the one called *Alien Abduction* written in the late 70s. A drawing of a creature was on the cover that looked very much like the ones he'd seen underground. He cracked it open and read all of two sentences before his thoughts were interrupted.

"What the heck is your dad having you study?" Jay heard an arrogant voice drift down from above him, making him flinch a little and raise his gaze to Ishmael's small, dark cranium, outlined with the glow of fluorescent lights. He glared at him through his wide, wire-framed lenses on his fat nose, then surveyed Jay's books with a disparaging, lopsided smirk that Jay would have loved to smack off. His redder than red lips shined bright, like lip gloss made of spit.

"Hi. Um, no." Jay feigned a smile, trying his best to hide his annoyance. "This isn't schoolwork. It's for fun."

Ishmael shifted his load of books to one arm. Jay tried not to look at the titles. Even so, he noticed the word 'Calculus.' Ishmael plucked up *The Alien Probes*, snarling at it as if he was a preacher and the literature pornographic. "*This* is for fun?"

Jay ripped the book out of his hands and placed it back on the table. "What are you doing here, studying for your next spelling bee? Or maybe trying to crack a secret code?" he said, his voice laced with mockery. With irritation, he recalled the bookshelf in Ishmael's room that held six huge, gleaming, cup-shaped trophies with 'National Spelling Bee Champion' carved above his name on each, along with the year it was earned.

"No," Ishmael sneered.

He'd known from the very beginning that the arrangement Aunt Vicki and Ishmael's mom had set up was a bad idea and was thankful he'd never have to step foot in Ishmael's house again. "You know, there's such a thing as a weekend. You can take a break sometimes."

"Yes. That may be true." Ishmael lifted his nose in the air and peered at Jay with judgment on his smug face. "But then I would only be about twice as intelligent as you. And that would suck."

Jay snarled, glancing back down at his book, hoping if he didn't give him eye contact, he'd disappear. "Idiot."

"Seriously?" Ishmael grew silent, still looming over him until Jay raised his head. Ishmael scowled at Jay with contempt, his eyebrows lifting in mock surprise. "You're calling me an idiot? *I'm* the one that tutored *you*."

Jay remembered all too well. Dad had needed someone to help Jay understand geometry, which was further proof he should have remained in public school in Jay's opinion. Aunt Vicki's solution was to call on the genius Ishmael. What a huge mistake that had been.

When Jay had shown him his geometry book, Ishmael all but scoffed at it. "I've been able to do those problems for years," he'd said, sitting on the bed while thumbing through Jay's textbook like he was reminiscing through an old photo album. What a nightmare.

Now Ishmael cleared his throat from above him. "Do you even know what my IQ is?"

"No, and I don't care. Don't you have somewhere you need to be?"

"194." Ishmael said each number loudly and deliberately. "What's yours?"

Jay sighed, squinting at him. "Would you go away?" Truth was he had no idea what his IQ was, but even if he did, he was sure he wouldn't have mentioned it.

"That's what I thought." Ishmael adjusted his books again, which he struggled with due to his lack of arm strength. "Have fun reading about your ancestors." He snorted and stomped off in his black tennis shoes, which he wore unfashionably with khaki shorts and black socks pulled up high, rounding off his overall geeky physique.

Jay rolled his eyes as he watched him go. "Jerk." Really, it was no wonder the guy didn't like Jay much. He couldn't blame him. And yet, he'd never failed to tick him off all the same.

After a couple of weeks of his Thursday visits to Ishmael's house, which was nothing if not sheer torture, he'd had enough. Outside of bragging, all Ishmael did was throw casual insults at him. Jay realized he did not, definitely *did not*, wish to be friends with this moron, acquaintances with him, or know him in any way, shape or form. So, he'd concocted a plan.

He knew it would have to be Ishmael's decision not to

go on with the arrangement or Aunt Vicki would never let him out of it. And this kid was having too much fun insulting him, practically making a game out of it, so that would probably never happen unless Jay interfered. So, on their fourth get together, after Ishmael asked Jay if he could teach him cursive with annoying, self-righteous piety, Jay told him he just wanted to sit on a director's chair along the back wall next to Ishmael's trophy case and read.

Of course, Ishmael wouldn't let him off that easily and when he started going on about his codes and how smart he was, Jay knew it was time. He'd "accidentally" knocked into his trophies, sending them to the floor, breaking at least half of them, some in several pieces. After doing it, seeing Ishmael's pathetic expression and how he cradled a broken piece of one of his spelling bee trophies like it was an injured puppy, he'd instantly felt bad. But by then it was too late.

He'd apologized, but Ishmael still sent him home and he'd never been invited back. Although it was mission accomplished, Jay still held a lot of guilt about it. It was true that Ishmael got on his nerves more than anyone he'd ever met. Frankly he couldn't stand the conceited jerk. Still, he couldn't shake the feeling that he'd done something wrong.

Now, as Jay sat in the library with the alien book open in front of him thinking about that day, he rested his chin on his fist, feeling a flicker of anger at himself. Had Ishmael really deserved what Jay had done? His eye caught Ishmael in the near distance by a bookshelf, talking to another nerdy guy with curly red hair and wire-framed glasses. Ishmael pointed at Jay, and the two of them giggled. Once they recognized that Jay spotted them, they turned to each other, laughed again and spun away.

Jay frowned and gritted his teeth. Actually, maybe he did deserve it. Just a little.

21

ALIEN RESEARCH

J ay couldn't help but question the mental stability of the men and women who claimed to see aliens in his newly checked out library books. *The Alien Probes* book was crazy stuff. He understood why people dismissed this kind of thing, thinking the witnesses were nuts. The book spoke about a lot of abuse and experimentation by aliens to its authors—a lot of probing, thus the name.

As he made his way back home, he examined the picture of the authors on the back cover—a married couple, both with wild gray hair, named Tan and Kim Lang. He skimmed their bios. "So they're the only ones who saw the aliens? No one else? That's messed up. Sounds like they're just a couple of wackos." He glanced back at their pictures. "Yeah, they totally look like it too."

The other two books, *True Stories of Alien Encounters* and *Alien Abduction,* were both filled with reports and testimonials from victims and bystanders. The stories were sketchy at best. People barely remembered what happened and were unsure of the details. Most of them had no memory of the abduction until years later. One even said his dentist found some kind of foreign substance underneath his wisdom teeth, and they couldn't figure out what it was. Once removed, he remembered everything about his disturbing encounter, like it had been a memory blocker.

In *True Stories of Alien Encounters*, a man reported a piece of metal had come out of his nose when he blew it into a tissue after he'd caught a bad cold. Friends of his had testified that he'd acted completely different once he removed the obstruction. However, conveniently, he'd thrown it away, leaving no evidence of its existence.

Many people had seen spacecraft resembling flying metal saucers, and some had even witnessed them sucking electricity out of power lines. There were accounts of children interacting with beings from other worlds, only they didn't remember the experience or didn't tell anyone about it until they were adults.

Jay decided he would read each story, no matter how outrageous they seemed. You never know what you could learn.

On his way home, he sat on a bench in the park and flipped through the book, *True Stories of Alien Encounters* by Dr. Ralph Peterson. Dr. Peterson was a psychiatrist and hypnotist who specialized in helping those who claimed to experience alien encounters. Some called him, *The Therapist to the Abducted*. The book was a compilation of stories he'd been told by his clients. One stuck out to Jay from the others, listed in the table of contents as:

Harper Brown and Mary Kagel, 1972

Brookfield, Colorado - Page 53

"Whoa, they're from here." He turned to page 53 and began to read.

Harper Brown and Mary Kagel

Harper Brown was born and raised in Brookfield, Colorado. At nineteen, he moved out of his parents' home and into a farmhouse on a plot of land they had gifted him. Shortly thereafter, he married a woman named Belinda, who passed two years later while giving birth to a stillborn child Harper named Sarah. He lived alone for the rest of his time in Brookfield, running his small farm until the day he disappeared on August 12, 1972, at the age of 24.

Mary Kagel was a widow and mother of a five-year-old boy living in Columbine Springs, Colorado when she disappeared from Brookfield on the same date. As far as anyone knew, she was fairly content and loved her son very much. The child seemed well rounded, healthy, and happy. Mary was the same age as Harper, and they had known each other in high school.

Mr. Brown told two of his ranch hands about his experiences with aliens while in his farmhouse, which always took place at night and had begun about a year after his darling wife died. He later recalled some other instances that occurred while he was in high school. One of his ranch hands, a man we will call John, was 78 years old when he retold this to me in a session. I am quoting him with his consent.

"Harper was a great man. All four ranch hands, myself
and three part-time helpers including my teenage son, really
enjoyed working with him. He was kind and generous and
attended Catholic mass most every Sunday that I knew him,
which was almost five years.

"He confided in me and my boy one day that he'd had a
strange dream, telling us he felt like he had floated out of his
second-floor bedroom window. In the dream, he was in a
room with a bunch of weird, gray-colored creatures with
huge black eyes, large heads, and skinny bodies. They took
blood from him and sperm, hair samples and even scraped
the inside of his mouth with something. None of it hurt at all,
and he said he couldn't move during the ordeal but was
conscious of what was going on around him. Like he was
awake and asleep at the same time. A few months afterward,
he informed me it had happened again, and that he thought it
wasn't a dream at all. He thought it was real.

"About three months before he disappeared, Harper was in a
car accident on the road just a fifteen-minute drive from the
farm. He'd hit a deer with his truck and rolled it. He was darn
lucky to have survived. His neck was fractured, and he broke
his arm. He was in the hospital for a little while with a
concussion. When he got out, he told me he'd remembered
something as soon as he woke up in the hospital. Something
that happened when he was in high school on a date. The girl
he'd gone on that date with was Mary Kagel, although I
didn't know that until after they'd both gone missing.

"He told me they'd seen a bright light as they were driving
down a dirt road that night and had stopped the car out of

curiosity. He didn't remember exiting the vehicle. The next memory he had was of the two of them in a small, white room with bright lights shining on them, making it hard to see. He concluded that they were on tables being examined by alien-looking creatures. The details were faded in his mind, but he somehow knew these beings were the same ones he'd recently come in contact with.

"They implanted something into his neck. He remembered that. Sure enough, he had a scar there. I'd never noticed it before, though, so I can't attest to where it came from. Might have happened in the car accident. But he swore up and down that they'd inserted an object there and that when he ran his hand over that spot, he could feel something. I wanted to believe him. But it was strange.

"A few months later, he announced he'd been in contact with Mary and asked her if she'd had similar experiences with aliens. She'd said she did not. However, she did remember vaguely seeing the light on the road those many years ago, but only after he told her about it. He mentioned she had a mark on her neck too, but she didn't recall having anything inserted there.

"Then, on August 12, 1972, when I got up early in the morning for work, he was nowhere to be found. I had a key to his house, and I went in, but nothing looked out of the ordinary. I knew something was wrong though. I lived in a ranch house on the property, and as far as I knew, he'd never spent the night anywhere but in his own bed. Plus, his truck was parked in the driveway. The next day, I called the police. I never saw him again.

"Couple days after this, I read in the paper that he'd run off with that girl, Mary Kagel. The police said she'd deserted her young son, Eugene, so they could go off together, even though anyone who knew her claimed she was crazy about that boy and extremely protective of him. Besides that, neither of them took a vehicle. To this day, I have no idea what really happened, but I've always been haunted by his stories of aliens."

This book fascinated Jay more so than the others, especially this chapter. What if these stories were true? Yes, they were bizarre and unbelievable, but after what Jay had seen, let's face it, anything was possible.

As Jay made his way down the street toward home, he thought about how strange it was that the underground creatures, the ones Nina called, "the Grays," resembled the aliens others claimed to see ever since the Roswell incident in 1947. Obviously other people had seen them like he had, whether their stories about abductions and probing were factual or not. It wasn't just science fiction. These were living, breathing beings. Beyond a shadow of a doubt, he knew—the aliens were real.

PART III

THE PROPHECY

22

A PLANNED MEETING

Vicki swept aside branches thick with green leaves as she made her way through the woods early that morning toward the regular meeting place. As the sun rose, the outline of the burnt house became visible through the trees, like a painting splashed with orange, purple, and blue. She never enjoyed coming here. Way too many painful memories were attached. But it was the only place he would meet her.

A squeal escaped her throat as a bug flew square into her face and she quickly swatted it away. She hated bugs, especially the flying kind. She never really got used to those. At least there weren't as many here in Colorado compared to other places because of the elevation, or so she'd been told. She had never been anywhere else.

There he was, the defined muscles in his arms pronounced beneath a tight dark green T-shirt and black pants, his hands resting on his hips. The sight of him stirred a flood of memories—some good, many not. For a moment it felt like no time had passed.

As she picked up her pace, she caught his eye. A smile spread across his face as he approached her with outstretched arms. "Sister!" he cried as she returned the embrace. He handed her a bag upon their release, which she gratefully accepted. "It's been so long."

"How are you, David? How are things in the Underground?"

"Everything is fine."

"I've missed you." She peered into the bag that contained the little yellow pills that helped her breathe on the outside. "Why so many?"

"I won't be back for a while."

"Longer than usual? Why?"

"We're getting closer." He placed his hands on her small shoulders. "It's almost time. I understand what to do now. It's becoming clearer to me every single day. We'll all be avenged. Soon, the prophecy will be complete." The last few times she'd seen David, he'd spoken of the prophecy, but wouldn't provide many details. She assumed this time would be no different.

His talk of freedom seemed too good to be true. "Oh David, you and your pipe dreams," she said, shrugging him off gently.

"You will see, Sister. None of it will be easy or free from danger, but we'll soon be released from the tyranny of the Grays."

Vicki squinted, looking deep into his eyes with suspicion. "This doesn't involve my family, does it?" She understood he had a mission, a vendetta, but if it was dangerous, she didn't want herself, Gene or especially Jay involved.

David's silence answered her question.

"No, I won't allow it." Vicki was tired of watching Jay get hurt. Her thoughts traveled to that horrible day when he was so small, not too long after his mother had died. "Do you remember what I told you about Jay? How he found my skin on the floor and screamed that I was dead, and all my blood gone? That really upset him. It traumatized him." For all she knew, he still suffered the effects. It made her tear up to think of it.

"Carelessness on your part, dear Sister."

"I'm aware. My point is, he had to see a psychiatrist... a doctor," she clarified after seeing his look of confusion. "And we had to take him out of school because I was afraid the Grays might try to harm him. He's been through enough already. Leave him be."

"I know you know this, Vicki." His hair hung just above one of his dark eyes, his brow raised high, revealing four distinct lines on his forehead, "But that's Tara's family, not yours."

"No," she screamed in a whisper, unable to contain her anger. "I made a promise!" She thrust a finger at him in defiance. "They are my family, and I need to know what you mean to do with Jay."

"I never mentioned Jay," he replied calmly, despite her near hysterics. "And you know I can't tell you the plan."

"Please. Hasn't this family suffered enough?" Vicki asked, knowing he was tip toeing around his words, trying to say them in just the right way as to not upset her. Only, it had the opposite effect because she knew him too well to be fooled. "No more. I won't let you. It's bad enough what I've had to do. How would Jay feel if he found out I planted the gun in his locker to get him removed from school? It would kill him." Vicki remained wracked with guilt, but also thankful she'd convinced the principal the gun was fake and to give it back to her without involving the police.

David threw his head back, clearly stunned. "I never advised you to do that. I didn't even want you to do that."

For a second, Vicki thought he might turn from her and walk away, and she placed a hand on his arm just in case. "I had to. He would never agree to leave school unless forced."

"This is not my problem," he said with a hard edge to his voice.

"You gave me the gun."

"Are you being serious?" He glared at her in disbelief. "I didn't know what you planned to do with it."

"You also didn't ask," she mumbled.

"Listen, don't blame me. I have to do what I have to do, no matter who's in danger. I'll put myself in the most danger, I don't care. Mary's prediction—"

"That does not involve Jay."

David tightened his lips and blinked. "That's your opinion."

"What? How can you say that?" He was most definitely hiding something, and his words only confirmed it.

He frowned at her. His dark, glassy eyes could sometimes take over her heart and make her feel any way he chose. More times than not, she was at their mercy. But not this time. She would simply not give in.

"I'm trying to end the suffering," he said. "Haven't *our* people suffered enough—*our* family? The time is now."

"For what?"

"I can't give you details. Not yet."

Vicki lowered her head and took in a deep breath. His secrets were driving her mad. No matter what she'd said or how many times she'd asked, he would never give her details. There was an obvious reason for his hesitance. It was because she wouldn't like it. But what could she do? Being disconnected from Stoneburrow, she had no say. She was nothing—a pawn. All she could do was try to influence the outcome. But if he wouldn't listen, then she was done. "You and that blasted prediction," she scolded, crumpling up the bag. "For all you know that woman was senile."

"I don't think so. Tara believed in the prophecy. You must feel it in your heart like I can. Don't you?"

"I want to believe, I do. It just sounds so dangerous, and frankly, unlikely."

David chuckled, shaking his head. "You and Kahl, by the Earth's core, you are so alike in your lack of trust."

"Who's Kahl?"

"From the Underground. I've mentioned him."

"I'm sure you haven't." He always seemed very careful about what he told her, and she was absolutely positive he'd never brought up this Kahl person before.

David blinked his eyes once. "It doesn't matter. The point is you need to trust me."

"You seem so sure about all this. I wish I was. You're so positive if you follow that prediction with precision, you'll free the people of Stoneburrow from the Gray's oppression. I do hope that's true, but at the same time, I don't want Jay to have any part in this. I can't lose him, too." Although she tried, she was unable to mask the panic in her voice.

"It'll be all right," he encouraged, as he approached

her and swiped her straight hair out of her eyes with the tips of his fingers. She peered up at him, tearful. "It must be done according to the prediction. We will be free. All of us."

"I just don't know if what you're doing is safe—for anyone."

David shook his head. "This must end now. The Grays cannot keep killing and destroying Units and ruling with no empathy. They would've killed you long ago if they'd found you. Thankfully, they think you're dead now or they'd still be after you. And they'd kill me too if they ever find out about my plans. You're worried about being safe? We're not safe now. We will never be safe with the Grays in charge. What do we have to lose?"

She pressed her lips together as she studied the man before her, trying to read his thoughts. In the past, she'd felt she knew him so well; now he seemed almost like a stranger. "We could lose a lot. I could lose Jay. I've already lost so much."

"It's not all about you, Vicki."

"I realize that. I'm only trying—"

"It's not all about you! Our window of opportunity is getting smaller and smaller. Your magic is getting stronger every day, but it's only a matter of time before they figure out the power of the Paragon and use it to their advantage to destroy everyone we love. We must act and we *will* act quickly." He cleared his throat with a look of impatience at Vicki's reluctance to comply. "Look, I have to go. I've been gone too long already." He turned to leave.

"Wait," she yelled after him, and he stopped. "What about this dog? Why is Nina hanging around Jay so much? Will you at least fill me in, since I helped you by enchanting the collar?"

"She's there to protect Jay. As I've said, I'm unable to tell you anything further. Goodbye, my sister." He turned to go.

"Nina is causing trouble for Jay, not protecting him. I feel bad because I helped you with this and now it's backfiring."

"It isn't backfiring." He pivoted, strolling backward with a grin on his face. "All is going according to plan."

"You keep mentioning this plan, yet you refuse to tell me anything."

"Sister," he said, half laughing. "I know you too well. If I told you, you'd try to stop it." With stealth, he darted away, disappearing into the trees.

A tear fell down Vicki's cheek, but it was in vain. She could do nothing. "Tara, forgive me." She caressed the red stone on her finger. Her thoughts traveled to Makk and the day he'd agreed to gift the Paragon to her years ago when she had to escape to survive the wrath of the Grays. The stone was the most glorious gift she'd ever received. What a blessing it had been in this world to heal the animals she loved so much with the power of this wonderful gem. But what a curse it had been as well.

She kissed it, missing her sister. Tara had an identical one that now hung around Jay's neck. If only he knew of its power. And yet, she hoped and prayed he never would discover it.

Vicki started for home, winding her way through the trees and thick foliage once again. The one and only thing Tara had asked of her was to keep her little family safe from the Grays—to keep them from doing to Tara's husband and child what they'd done to Tara. Vicki had accomplished this feat for a time. Now, it all seemed to be unraveling, and she was unable to do anything to stop it. She had a bad feeling about all of this.

"Why can't I keep them safe?" All she knew was she had to continue to try. She had no choice.

23

TRICKED

His shoes swished as he shuffled along the sidewalk from the library to Nina's spot, but Jay barely noticed. His mind was on the alien books to the point of obsession. He wanted to get Nina's thoughts on what it all meant. At the very least, she might find the books interesting. He plopped himself down beside the entrance to the tunnels, expecting her to be there or pop out of the hole, but she did not.

After a while, he grew impatient and cracked open one of his library books to distract him. He found himself drawn again to the story about Mary Kagel and Harper Brown in *True Stories of Alien Encounters*. He'd read it at least twenty times. Now, as he tried concentrating, the words seemed empty and the pages blank.

He dropped the book and rubbed his tired eyes. "I don't get it. Where is she today?" It made no sense. Every time Jay had passed this spot, Nina had been there, watching him. Now that he actually wanted to find her, she was nowhere to be seen. Was she avoiding him?

Discouraged, irritated, and tired of waiting, Jay considered getting up and going home, until a thought struck him. Every time he walked down the street, Nina was already there, like she knew he was coming before he did. He scanned the area, careful not to make any sudden moves. Something shifted behind a shrub about fifteen feet away. Was that black fur, or just his imagination?

"Nina?" He got to his feet and crept toward the bush. "Is that you? Why are you hiding?" Her form sat still as stone as Jay crept toward her. "What's wrong?"

He sat down in front of it, his legs folded beneath him. "You'll have to come out sooner or later." He wondered if it wasn't her at all—that sitting in solitude behind the bushes for over an hour had driven him mad. Just as doubt crept in, the bush began rustling.

Nina stepped out and padded toward him, her tail tucked between her legs and her head hung low, avoiding his gaze. "What's up?" he asked her. She seemed to gesture with her eyes to the hole. "Oh yeah, you have to take off your collar to talk to me, huh?"

Nina nodded but didn't move as Jay expected her to. Instead, she motioned to the hole again.

"Ah," he said with realization. "Really, Nina. I'd rather not. Can't you go down, take off the collar, and come back up like last time?" If he never went down that dreaded pipe again, it would be too soon.

Nina stood still, staring at him in silence.

"Oh, man." His heart dropped into his stomach.

She sat down curling her tail around her, unmoving, insisting.

"Fine," he agreed with no enthusiasm. "I must be

nuts." He stood and made his way to the cover, extending his hand. "You first."

Over the bushes, his eye caught two girls around his age strolling down the sidewalk. They glanced at him, giggling, a high-pitched, annoying sound that turned Jay's face a bright, hot red. "That kid is playing some weird game with his dog!" one of them squealed. "He's like, talking to it!" And the other said, "What a freak!" Jay looked down at Nina, biting his lower lip. She responded with what seemed to be a frown but must have been his imagination. Then she nudged the cover open with her nose and disappeared inside as graceful as a cat.

Before following her, Jay remembered his books and stowed them away inside a bush so no part was detectable. He shined his light inside the hole, watching in awe as Nina climbed all the way down, using her mouth and her arms to grab the rungs. She gracefully landed on her feet at the bottom like she'd done it a million times.

As he began his descent, he shut the cover above him and darkness took over. Sweat broke out over his body, and yet he was suddenly cold. "Don't leave me," he called down to her through the blackness with a bit of panic in his voice. He received a strange bark in return that closely resembled a cough but was clearly not human.

His shoes made a loud, echoing sloshing sound as they hit the wet floor, and his socks immediately soaked up the dirty water. The light from his flashlight hit the empty turn of the pipe, revealing Nina wasn't there. He sighed deeply, regretting it as he took in the foul, cold, musty air. "Nina," he cried between coughs. He knew she couldn't be far but wondered if she'd taken off as she had before. "Nina!" he called again.

"Over here," a voice returned to him, not far away, sounding like someone who perhaps had a cold or was getting over laryngitis. He trudged forward through the ankle-deep water until he arrived at the part of the pipe that opened to the larger section. He laid his flashlight on the dry concrete and pulled himself up two feet and out of the dirty liquid.

While stomping his feet to remove as much water as possible, he sensed a presence and picked up his light to shine it to the right of him. A black dog appeared, standing upright with a human head. He came close to screaming and might have done so if his brain had been slower in registering that the head belonged to Nina. Her long blonde hair reached down to the dog's tail, and her familiar light blue eyes remained unchanged, glowing in the dim light. With human hands covered in thin, black fur, she held the blue collar in front of her chest, the tags dangling like an ugly necklace. He could snap her picture and post it all over social media and no one would believe it was real. "Wow!" was all he managed to croak out. She returned the exclamation with a sheepish look.

He felt weird, as if he were watching someone dress, so he flicked off the flashlight and turned away. Good thing, he realized afterward, because the dog version of Nina wasn't wearing clothes. After her transformation, she would have to put on her burlap shirt and dark pants which lay crumpled at her feet.

"Okay, I'm done," she told him, her voice youthful and sweet as it had been before. She shielded his light with her hands, wearing her usual outfit, her feet bare. Her short, worn-out brown boots sat neatly beside her, the black socks tucked inside them, alongside her backpack.

"Sorry," he said after noticing the light was blinding her. He shifted it slightly to the left to aim it on the wall beside her head. "Why were you hiding?"

The whites of her large eyes shone bright in the flash-light's glow. "I was watching you."

"Watching me reading? Why?"

"It's just what I do."

Jay lifted his brow. "Well, that's disturbing."

As she sighed, her bottom lip appeared to take over her mouth. "I feel bad, Jay."

"Bad?" Jay stepped closer until they were only a few feet apart, drawing in her musty smell. It reminded him of the thrift store Aunt Vicki sometimes took him to when he was younger and money was tight.

"I may have revealed too much about me—about my world."

"Too much? We've barely spoken at all. Last time I saw you, we talked for like two minutes. Why do you think that?"

"It was longer than two minutes and I shouldn't have talked to you at all." Her eyes dropped to her pale, bare feet, glistening with dirty water in the soft light, her toes small and delicate. "You should have never followed me."

"Look, I won't say anything, if that's what you're worried about. Honestly, if I tried, I'd just end up looking like an even bigger joke." He rested the fingertips of his left hand on his chest. "You can totally trust me." Who was he going to tell? He had no friends. Anyone watching him would know that.

"It's not your loyalty that I question. It's your safety."

"Safety? What're you talking about?" He glanced at her from the corners of his eyes, wondering if he should be worried.

"Well, if I told you that, I'd be telling you too much again."

"Is it the creatures? I mean, the Grays? Are they dangerous?"

"It's complicated."

"I'm not afraid," he told her, mostly to ease her mind. He didn't know if that was a fact or not. What he needed was more information to make that statement either accurate or a load of crap.

"You don't understand what you're saying. You have no idea."

"Then why don't you tell me? I'll make up my own mind."

Nina bit the side of her lip and fidgeted with her hands. "Well, the truth of it is, we could use your help. You might prove useful."

"Useful? What am I, a hammer or something? And who's this 'we' stuff?"

"Sorry. I don't mean it that way. It's just, I wish I could explain, but if I do and you say no, it's too late. I won't be able to take back what I tell you."

Jay shook his head, his lips slightly parted. "I have no freakin' clue what you're talking about."

"Like I told you, it's complicated. And risky."

"It's okay. I give you my consent. Just tell me. After that, if I'm in danger, it's my own fault, okay? Your conscious can be clear."

"That's easy to say. You may not feel that way later."

"Tell me already," Jay whined, trying to hide his impatience with no success.

"You sure?"

He glared at her. "Dude."

"Okay. We can talk. But not here." Nina threw her bag over her shoulder by its strap, picked up her boots by the shoestrings, and grabbed his hand with her small one, pulling him down the tunnel.

"Hold up." He dug his heels in, stopping her.

"What? You said you were sure."

"Right. Still, it would be nice to know where you plan to take me."

"It's a secret place. We can't talk up there, as you know." She pointed upward. "And it's not safe here. Follow me and I'll show you."

"But what about the...you know, those things?" His voice shook as he pointed down the tunnel where the two beasts hid in the darkness.

"Don't worry." She leaned down and rifled through her bag. When she popped back up, she produced the flesh-colored fruit that looked like a freakish artichoke. "We only need to pass the crocodile, that's it. I have clothes hidden for you up here too."

"Clothes?"

"You'll need to blend in, of course. The Grays make us dress alike." Nina smiled at him, her yellowish teeth glowing in the light.

"You played me, didn't you?" He squinted at her and a blush crept across her cheeks.

"Played?"

"You knew I would go with you."

"No. I just believe in being prepared," she said matter-of-factly, shrugging.

Jay gave her a tight-lipped smile. She was good. By the time she was done with him, he'd practically begged to go with her, hadn't he?

She snatched his hand once more and started off without another word as he trailed her with reluctance. "Well, at least *she's* prepared," he whispered under his breath. If only he himself was. He couldn't escape the feeling that maybe he had agreed to this too soon.

24

BUGS AND WORMS

J ay felt small in his new attire, which comprised a black burlap shirt, black pants, and worn, scuffed-up black boots. The clothes fit him all wrong. The pants were too long and the waist too wide. He had to roll the cuffs several times and was thankful for the belt Nina had given him, or they'd be around his ankles. The shirt seemed made for a larger man who at least had some muscle to his frame, and his feet shifted uncomfortably in the boots.

Even though it wouldn't be visible, Nina had him draw the symbol on his ankle again in case the Gray authorities stopped him, which he prayed wouldn't happen. In some ways, those things scared him even more than the crocodile and the snake which could at least be tamed.

Nina walked ahead in the glow of Jay's flashlight. "Okay, we're taking a different route so, like I told you, we'll only have to deal Chompy."

Jay raised an eyebrow. "Chompy?"

"Yeah, the crocodile."

Jay exhaled and threw his head back. "Wonderful. It has a name."

"Well, it fits, doesn't it?" she responded in a high pitch.

"Hey, wait a minute," Jay said, which didn't cause Nina to slow her pace at all. "What about the third trap?" She seemed to ignore him. "You know, the water one? The one you forgot to tell me about but let me find out on my own?" he reminded her with irritation.

She stopped, bending over, searching for something. "Step behind me a little," she commanded, and he did. She flipped open her bag and pulled out a small, black spray can, shaking it vigorously.

Jay spotted a thin yellowish line across the path. "That's the one." Nina squatted down and sprayed the clear, unknown substance on the side of the wall. The line disappeared. "I thought it was string or something. How did I trip over a beam of light?"

"It's enchanted."

"Enchanted? What does it mean when you say stuff is enchanted? And who's enchanting these things?"

Nina exhaled. "I can't say. That'll have to wait until we get there."

Jay's curiosity was strong, feeling like an itch he couldn't quite reach. It didn't seem she was going to tell him much, yet he continued to ask questions. "Why wasn't it there when I was following you?"

"I sprayed it when I went through. It wears off, but not for a while." She threw the pack over her shoulder. "Then it comes back."

"Ah. Thanks so much for telling me about it," he

mocked. They started walking again, her in front of him as before.

"Well, I *did* tell you that you had everything you needed to get through the traps."

"Yeah, but I didn't. I didn't know anything about that beam. Plus, I didn't have that spray junk, whatever it is."

Nina turned over her shoulder, her blonde hair whipping around her head. "It would've been impossible for me to tell you where it was, especially since we were running out of time. I knew you'd be fine. You're a fast runner."

"How do you know that?"

"I know almost everything about you, Jay. I've been watching you for a while."

It felt weird to have this virtual stranger, someone he knew nothing about, know so much about him, especially since her information was obtained by spying on him.

"I also know about the girl you were talking to. Lydia?"

"What about her?"

"You like her," she sang.

Jay frowned, defensive. "No, I don't!" He wasn't sure if "like" was the right word after all she'd done to him. He definitely had feelings. But he wasn't about to admit to it to this kid. Especially since he wasn't even sure what he felt anymore.

"Someday, Lydia, I will thank you in person with a kiss," Nina mocked.

Jay felt his face grow hot. "What? You heard that?"

Nina giggled a sweet little girl laugh.

His body tightened up as anger snuck in. "That's

pretty creepy, you know." Nina didn't respond, but Jay sensed she was still smiling. "Why were you following me around, anyway? It's called stalking and not cool." He couldn't help wondering if she was jealous. Maybe she had a crush on him.

"I had to be sure we could trust you."

"Yeah, right," Jay huffed, still thinking his theory was the most likely.

"Why do *you* stalk that girl, Lydia?"

"I don't stalk her!" Jay stood up straight, his chest out, scowling. "Besides, she likes me."

"It doesn't seem like it to me."

"Well, she does. I know for a fact. She brought my cap back after Brian punched me. That's gotta mean something."

Nina laughed again, throwing her hand to her mouth.

"What?"

"That was me."

"You?" Jay stopped for a second, remembering how moist his cap was. "Aw, come on, dude. That was dog slobber?"

"Sorry." She seemed torn between feeling guilty and trying not to laugh.

"Whatever." He attempted to suppress his disappointment. This was the only nice thing Lydia had ever done for him, and the only reason he thought she might like him, at least a little. Without that, he was left with nothing. In truth, she probably hated him. She'd set him up to get pummeled by Brian, which seemed to prove it. Man, he was an idiot.

"I didn't mean to make you feel bad," she said, her tone now softened.

"It's chill," he lied, then cleared his throat, making a sound like a mini explosion in the cramped space. Even though it came from his own mouth, it still made him flinch. "What is that spray stuff anyway?" he asked, changing the subject.

"It's something my mentor developed."

"Your mentor? Who's that?"

"You'll meet him," Nina answered, her voice calm, the opposite of how Jay was feeling. "His name is David."

"Who's David? Another kid?"

Nina scuffed her feet along the floor of the tunnel, occasionally stepping over a stalagmite or rock, her steps loud, echoing. "No, he's older. Kind of like a dad to me. He wants to meet you." The words took a bite out of his heart, and he wanted to tell her to forget the whole thing. Taking him underground was one thing, but meeting others, especially adults, made him uncomfortable.

She must have picked up on it. "Don't worry. You can trust David."

"But why does he want to meet me?"

"I told him all about you and he wants to, that's all," she said as if it were no big deal. Jay wanted to believe her and feel confident, but skittish was all he could muster as he walked down the cold, dark underground passageways to meet a strange man alongside a girl who could turn into a dog. *Weird.*

"You shouldn't be afraid of David. He's on our side."

"Our side?" As he looked at her profile, he found himself curious to learn more about her and her life underground. "There are sides?"

"Of course. Units and Grays. The Grays haven't been kind to the Units for at least as long as I've been alive."

"Are you scared of them?"

"Oh, yes." She stopped and turned to face him, her eyes growing large. "You would be also if you knew anything about them."

"Great." He blinked rapidly with uncertainty. "Is it too late to change my mind?"

"Really? Too afraid to go on?"

"No." He shook his head. "No, I'm good." But he was afraid. Petrified, in fact. Maybe it was his ego that kept him marching forward. Regardless, he had decided to follow her wherever she planned to take him, and wasn't about to back down because of fear.

Nina continued with Jay right behind. "Don't worry. It's safe where we're going."

"Where are we going again?"

"It's a secret place, even further under the earth than we are now. One that very few know about."

Before he could ask for more details, two glowing red eyes appeared in the distance and a sound like a failed car starting filled the air. It made the hair on the back of Jay's neck stand on end. As soon as they got close enough, Nina tossed the fruit to Chompy like it was old hat. It appeared to recognize her and to expect the flesh-colored fruit. Instead of going straight as Jay had before, they turned left into the crocodile's nest while it feasted on its prize on the other side.

They continued through the new path for a few minutes before Jay spoke again. "When you were a dog, didn't Brian hurt you? I mean, you seemed pretty messed up after he smashed you into that wall."

"Yes, he did. I was in a lot of pain. Your Aunt Vicki did something to me."

"What?"

"I'm not sure." She shook her head. "All I know is I passed out and the next thing I knew, I woke up outside by the entrance and I was fine. I mean, completely healed. Nothing broken and no pain."

"That's strange." What had Aunt Vicki done? Short of magic, was there anything that could take away pain and repair broken bones like that? And she left Nina by the entrance to the underground world? How did she know to do that? "Intense."

"Intense?"

"I mean, that's interesting."

"I thought so."

"It's pretty much impossible for anyone to heal that quickly. How did she do that?"

Nina shook her head again. "I don't know."

"Do you know Aunt Vicki?"

"Do you mean, are we friends?" She scrunched her face as if Jay had asked something preposterous.

"I guess so."

"No. I've never spoken to her."

"Well, she seems to know about you."

"She knows I exist." Nina ticked her head to the side and shrugged a shoulder. "She has ties to the Underground."

Jay stopped in his tracks, throwing his hand in front of her. "Ties? What ties?" The fact that Aunt Vicki knew about the civilization under the earth cleared up all the mysteries behind why she hadn't tried harder to protect Nina in her dog form. But how was Aunt Vicki connected to it? He had to know.

"Jay, you'll need to wait, okay? I know it's hard. We'll talk about all this with David once we get there."

Once again on the move, he mumbled, "Then, why say anything at all?"

"'Cause you keep on asking," she murmured back.

"How much further?" he whined, feeling like an annoying kid in the backseat. *Are we there yet?* He wished he could take back the words once spoken, especially when she didn't answer and let out a heavy sigh.

After a while, she stopped. "Okay, here." She motioned to a dark hole in the bottom of the wall. "We go down. It's only a small drop." She began squeezing her body through legs first, no trouble, as Jay watched with trepidation. Her blonde head disappeared into the shadows, and he heard the soft thud of her landing.

He mimicked her, shoving both legs inside. It was a tight fit, and a wave of fear crept in. What if he got stuck? What would they do if that happened? Let him stay there until he lost weight like on the Winnie the Pooh show he used to watch when he was little? "For real?" The image of someone drawing a face on his butt while they waited for him to shrink like in the cartoon flashed through his mind. His lungs began to close at the mere thought.

He didn't, however, have a problem. Once his torso slipped down, his feet landed on a small rock ledge, then he jumped three feet to the ground, which appeared to be constructed of hard clay.

"That wasn't so bad, right?" Nina said as he brushed the dirt and clay off his clothes.

"Could have been worse."

"Yeah, well, I hate to tell you, but it will get a little worse."

Jay was afraid to ask. "What do you mean?" The air was warmer here, thick with humidity, and his lungs felt tight. There didn't seem to be much air circulation. He rubbed his chest to ease the pressure.

Seeming to have read his mind, Nina left his question unanswered and reached into her bag once more, pulling out another can, which looked similar to the one she'd used to defuse the trap. She flipped off the cap, making a loud pop that echoed throughout the darkness, and attached a long, thin straw to the tip.

"What's that?" Jay asked.

"Open your mouth wide and stick your tongue out. It gets hard to breathe down here. This will help."

Jay obeyed, feeling his gag reflex give way as she stuck the straw all the way to the back of his throat and sprayed. He made a wrenching sound. Thankfully, nothing came up.

"Breathe, don't cough," she suggested. "Or we'll have to do it again."

He stifled it as best he could. "That's nasty!" he hissed, then coughed after breathing in and out two or three times, unable to hold it back any longer. He felt his lungs relax, taking away the tight feeling and replacing it with cleansing oxygen.

"Sorry. I know it tastes terrible. That's why we put it in the back, so it doesn't touch the tongue as much." She sprayed her own throat, then replaced the cap with a loud click and dropped it back into her bag as she breathed deeply.

They began walking once more through the new passageway, about half the width of the one they had just come from. The rock walls were more colorful, with red and orange running through the rocks and stalactites hanging from the ceiling. Stalagmites shot up here and there, and the path was quite tight in places.

When it opened up to its widest point, Nina stopped, extending her hand for Jay to do the same. "All right, this is what I meant about it getting worse. There's a trap, okay? And it's scary, but we can get through it."

Jay clicked his tongue. "Fantastic. What is it?" The tunnel seemed to go on forever and was wider than the one they'd just come from.

"It's bugs and worms. They can hurt you, but we can outrun them. You're fast, as I am."

"Um. Hold up. Bugs and worms?"

She sighed with shakiness in it, then pulled out a ruler-shaped stick from her pack with a bright pink neon stripe painted on the tip.

"What's that?"

"It doesn't matter. Look, just follow me. I'm not positive what trips off this trap. I don't know how to beat it except to outrun it. It only trips when you go this way, down this tunnel. If we went around the other way, we could have avoided it, but we would've had to go through the Great Room, which we don't have time for. Not to mention, if we get caught by the authorities, it'll be a lot worse than being suffocated and eaten by these bugs."

"Suffocated? Eaten? Suffocated and eaten by bugs. Is that what you said? What could possibly be worse than that?" Jay felt his knees grow weak.

"We'll have to be brave and just get through it. Don't panic and trust me." The nervousness in her voice did nothing to calm him. "And don't look back, okay?" She blinked her long, thick eyelashes, triggering a memory of what Aunt Vicki had said about Mom's eyelashes and how thick they were. Why the heck he was thinking about eyelashes at a time like this? "We can do it. We'll be fine."

Jay fidgeted with his hands to keep them from shaking. He wasn't afraid of bugs, but he wasn't fond of them either, especially spiders. Spiders were the worst. And yet, spiders don't suffocate or eat you.

"I'll need your flashlight." She held out her small hand to accept it. "It's brighter than anything I have."

With reluctance, he handed it over, almost telling her he'd decided to turn back and get the heck out of there. But something, maybe curiosity, pressed him forward. Besides, she said it would be fine, right? What could go wrong? He gulped hard enough to make a noise.

"Since we don't know when they'll appear, you'll just have to run fast. Run and don't stop until I tell you to."

"How many bugs are we talking about here?"

With that, Nina bolted down the tunnel, the light bobbing up and down in front of her. Less than half a second later, Jay was on her heels. She was fast. Almost as fast as he was. He could have passed her up but didn't because she had the flashlight. Plus, he had a hard time running in his large boots and this was not an ideal time to trip.

They ran for a while, maybe for two or three minutes. The only sound Jay heard was the clomping of their boots on the hard clay floor, their rapid breathing, and the echoes amplifying it all. He wondered if the bugs weren't actually coming. Perhaps Nina had been messing with him.

As he speculated how much longer they would have

to keep up the pace, he heard an unfamiliar noise. It sounded like a billion small feet running along with them, which he assumed was exactly what it was, though he didn't have the guts to turn and investigate.

"Here!" Nina yelled as the light disappeared from the path. She dropped onto her hands and knees and thrust the stick under what appeared to be a door hidden in the wall, much like the one he'd come across when he first discovered her underground world.

Jay snatched the flashlight from the ground and made a huge mistake. He shined it into the tunnel behind them to find a sick, blackish cloud of bugs lining the walls several inches thick on all sides. They were about two hundred and fifty feet away, if he were to guess, and moving quickly. His eyes doubled in size as he gazed upon this terrifying sight, unable to look away. The earth itself seemed to tremble at the combined force of their trillions of little legs.

He resisted the urge to grab her up by the arm and pull her back into a running pace away from harm. Yet, he had to trust that she knew better than he did. "Oh, please!" she yelled at the door, pushing the stick under the crack on the floor as far as it would go, pulling it to the left, then to the right.

"What?" he shouted over the thundering of the bugs, out of breath and near the panic stage. "What!"

"The stupid Door Unit isn't paying attention!" She moved the stick all around, sounding like she was crying. "Is he asleep or what? Wake up!" she screamed, her voice nearly drowned out by the commotion behind them.

Jay began banging his fist on the door with one hand. Not his best idea. He cringed as it shot up with pain and shined the light back on the bugs. As they approached, the creatures came into focus. A variety of roach-like insects mixed with centipedes—and unfortunately, spiders—crawled among other unidentifiable things, all swarming steadily nearer. He could now make out giant worm-like creatures with huge teeth slithering alongside them. He fought the desire to bang on the rock again, not caring anymore if he broke his hand in the process as long as someone opened the freakin' door.

"Wake up!" Nina screamed again.

The bugs were less than fifty feet away now. Along with the eerie sound of a thundering bug stampede came a horrible squishy noise—one he'd never heard before. They were done for, and Jay knew it. This was the end. These things would suffocate and eat them, like Nina said. He wanted to close his eyes to prepare for it but couldn't make his eyelids shut no matter how he willed them too.

"Wake up!" Nina yelled again. "Oh please! For the sake of the queen!"

Jay wanted to yell for help along with her, but he found himself unable to move his gaping mouth to form words. Instead, a scream of sheer terror exploded from somewhere inside him and escaped his throat. Although it was loud, it could barely be heard over the trillions of little legs charging toward them.

25

ISSUES WITH THE DOOR UNIT

To Jay's surprise, a thin red glow lit up in the crack of the door. Relief surged through him, sharp and fleeting, then vanished. The door was opening too slowly, and the creatures were closing in fast. He grabbed the sleeve of Nina's shirt, the flashlight still focused on the bugs stampeding toward them, growing closer by the second. "Get up! We need to run!"

"There's no time!" she shouted as he yanked her to her feet.

Before Jay knew what happened, the bugs quickly covered Nina's back as she began to scream, closing her eyes tight. The creeping monsters swallowed her frame with their long legs, crawling around her and over her hair into her face, turning her into a dark mass of squiggling bugs. There was no time to be afraid. The only emotion he felt at that moment was an intense feeling to protect her. With it, something inside him jumped—an electricity. Maybe his heart falling out of his chest. And then a miracle—out of nowhere. He reached out and touched her. Before she all but disappeared in the blackness of their grotesque bodies, a bright crimson light flashed and the bugs flew off and burst into flames, their crispy remains landing several feet away. The creatures along the walls closest to them smoldered, curled up, and died. Even though a good number of them had been destroyed, there seemed to be an endless supply, scrambling over the dead to reach their meal.

The door opened wider, illuminating them in red light. Nina made a noise that sounded like laughing, although he must have imagined it. No way he could have heard anything over the thundering sound of these horrible things approaching coupled with the loud music playing on the other side of the door. He pushed her inside, and she fell in a heap on the floor. As he squeezed himself through, more of the creatures covered his left arm.

"Shut it! Shut it!" some deep male voices yelled. The music quieted as all the red glowing faces turned their direction. Pain stabbed at Jay's arm in about twenty to thirty different spots, then a lot of slapping. Some brown thing, like a mixture of a silverfish and a lizard, slithered up his arm with amazing speed, crawling right up to his face. It was about a foot long from its nose to the tip of its tail. Jay craned his head back as it opened its weird lizard-like mouth, perhaps aiming for his nose. Someone knocked it off with such a force that it skidded along the floor flailing its legs and came to a stop right in front of a lady who promptly stomped on it, making its guts shoot out to the side of her black boot.

"Take that!" She moved her brown frizzy hair away from her face with a twitch of her head, revealing a look of rage and satisfaction at the creature she'd just obliterated.

Several people were still swatting bugs off him and stomping on the ground. "Did we get them all?" a man asked, along with another, "I think so." Roaches, spiders, and other things, some Jay had never seen before, lay dead next to their greenish innards splattered around the doorway.

Some men standing nearby helped Nina get to her feet. "Did you fall asleep?" she asked innocently, out of breath. Her cheeks were wet with tears, and she wiped them off with the tips of her fingers.

"I went to the bathroom," a young man said, who Jay presumed was the Door Unit. He was tall and gangly, had curly unmanageable brown hair that added at least a couple of inches to his height, and a long, skinny face. As he spoke, his massively crooked teeth glowed orange in the light.

"The bathroom?" another man responded from behind them in a gruff, dry sounding voice, clearly appalled as he strutted up to where they all stood. He was short. A lot shorter than the Door Unit and about an inch shorter than Jay. His head was large, and he had straight brown hair combed back. A bit of gray at the temples glowed crimson in the light. Bags hung under his eyes, and he had two deep creases on each side of his mouth with four or five more on his forehead. Other than his largish head, he appeared very normal—like any adult Jay might have seen at the library or passing him in an SUV as he made his way down the sidewalk. "What are you going to the bathroom for?"

The Door Unit's dark, bushy eyebrows formed into a frown. "I don't know. I had to go."

"You're supposed to have someone watch the door before you go anywhere! You know that! What's wrong with you?"

"It took me only a second."

The short man's scowl intensified. "Well, that second could have cost these two kids their lives, Galt. For the love of the queen! What were you thinking? Look at the mess you've made!"

Galt's face fell. His defensiveness gone, and he stared at the floor like a little kid being scolded, unable to keep eye contact. "I'm sorry."

"You should say sorry to Nina and her friend here. What's your name?" he asked, shifting his focus to Jay.

"Jay," he replied in a quiet voice.

"Right, Jay. Mine's Kahl, by the way." He stuck his hand out to shake, and Jay obliged. Then the man turned his attention back to Galt. "You know David would kill you if anything happened to Nina."

Galt plopped himself on a chair against the wall, looking discouraged and guilty, leaving Jay to wonder why they were so afraid of David. Maybe he should be as well.

Kahl scanned Jay up and down once. "You're new to the UU, aren't you?" Jay responded with a nod. "You're with Nina, so I trust you and all, but you still need to meet with David."

Jay turned to Nina with uncertainty. She nodded once, her expression giving him no reason for concern, which eased his mind a bit.

"And you need to get some ointment on those bites."

He motioned with his head to Jay's arm, which was now red and bumpy. Nina had some identical marks on her face, and he was sure her back was probably covered. "You're about to get very itchy."

A kid about Jay's age rushed up and tugged on Kahl's sleeve. His dark hair stuck out in uneven tufts, like he'd cut it himself. He wore the same style of shirt as Nina, though his was dark blue and looked a size too big, hanging awkwardly on his thin frame. There was an anxious energy about him, like a coil wound too tight as he shifted from foot to foot and interrupted in a high, whiny voice. "I was about to leave."

"Well, you can't now. We got bugs out there!" Kahl yelled.

The kid tightened his fists, a ball of nervous energy. "But I'm late for my shift!"

"What?" Kahl squinted at him. "That's your problem, boy! I'm not letting those things in here!"

"Snopes!" the kid barked, throwing an empty plastic cup on the hard floor. It cracked loudly before he kicked it across the room.

"Pick that up immediately," Kahl ordered. "And watch your language!" He shook his head in annoyance. "Have you all lost your minds?" he asked the entire room, then shouted to someone behind Jay, "I need a fast one, Units! We got bugs!"

Someone from behind the bar answered, "You got it."

"Don't worry. The vibration from the music will drive them away shortly," Kahl told the kid in a less than comforting tone. "Just sit tight."

The boy made a face of annoyance and whimpered, "But, I'm late already!"

"Well, I guess you'll have to deal with it. You plan better. Give yourself more time next time," he lectured.

It did little good as the kid appeared to grow more irritated the more Kahl talked. "Why did you all have to come through this door, anyway? Huh? Shucks!" the boy yelled at Jay and Nina, his voice squeaking midway through the first sentence.

"Calm yourself," Kahl instructed. "Go sit next to Galt. He'll let you know when you can leave."

As they bickered, Jay glanced around the room. It resembled any night club you might see in the movies with an empty dance floor and red lights shining on it from above. Along the back was a bar carved into the rock and behind it, lit up with white lights, were label-less bottles in all kinds of shapes and colors.

To the right were five small, round tables with chairs, half of them occupied. About fifty people were in the room, and they all looked normal except for their clothes. They wore burlap shirts in various colors, as Jay himself now wore. He would have never imagined, as they trudged through the frightening, trap-infested tunnels, that Nina was taking him to a party.

Kahl, who was observing Jay, perhaps with suspicion, cut short his thoughts. "That's an interesting name there, Jay," He stood up as tall as possible to attain eye level, getting right up into his face as if searching for something in it. "You spell that J-A-Y- E?"

"No, J—"

Nina interrupted, grabbing Jay's hand. "Yes. That's right, Kahl. We'll talk to David, don't worry."

"Where you from, *Jaye*?" Kahl called to him as they darted to the back. Loud music coming from somewhere he couldn't locate drowned out Nina's response, although Jay wasn't sure she even said anything. It was a Madonna song he'd heard before, and the quick techno beat filled the whole room with energy. People appeared to have forgotten all about the two of them stumbling in and began dancing where the lights from the ceiling shined the brightest from above.

Nina led Jay around the back to a room with an entrance covered up by a brown curtain. As they rushed by, a man behind the bar wearing a black T-shirt stared at Jay with dark, hollow eyes. He recognized him as the same man who had caused the distraction with Yag when Jay first stumbled into the Great Room. Besides that, Jay thought he'd seen him before, although he couldn't quite put his finger on where.

The man's gaze followed Jay without a hint of emotion. There was something about him that made Jay uneasy. For one thing, it was hard to tell if his expression conveyed anger, curiosity, or indifference. For another, as Jay looked into his eyes, he felt as though the man was peering into his very soul.

A strong, icy shiver traveled throughout his body.

26

FREEING THE UNITS

"I know this is all weird for you, Jay," Nina said, talking extra loud over the booming music filtering in through the thick, brown curtain, the only thing separating them from the party going on behind it. They settled onto two wooden stools in the small, chilly room surrounded by orange rock walls. In each corner, a candle burned along a ledge built within the rock, the light a pleasant change from the harsh red glow that had begun to irritate Jay's eyes.

"That's an understatement." His arm itched terribly. A few bumps decorated it from bites he'd sustained. He scratched at them with desperation, receiving no relief.

Nina also attempted to scratch her back, seeming frustrated as she couldn't quite reach it, squirming in her seat. "Yeah, well, it's all normal everyday stuff for me."

"You've got a weird and interesting idea of normal," Jay told her as she nodded.

"I guess so." Nina looked very young with her blonde

hair falling around her shoulders and her pigeon-toed feet inside worn brown boots resting on the bar at the bottom of her stool. She had very smooth white skin and chubby cheeks. Even though she seemed innocent, it was hard to believe she was just a kid. She certainly didn't talk like any kid he knew. "An old soul," Aunt Vicki would have called her.

Nina opened her eyes wide. "Tell me how you did that, Jay."

"Did what?"

"How did you get those bugs off me? Do you have a weapon?"

"A weapon?" He scrunched his face. "No."

"Where did the red light come from? After it flashed, the bugs flew off and exploded."

Jay pictured the bugs crawling up her arms, her neck, even her face, smothering the air out of her. He couldn't move, powerless to do anything. Then, just as fast as they came, the red light blasted through them, throwing them off in flames, allowing him to breathe again. "I don't know." He was as perplexed by it as she was. "It wasn't me. I thought it came from you."

"If you didn't do it, and I didn't do it, who did?"

He shrugged. "Maybe someone from behind the door?"

Nina's brow narrowed. "I don't think so."

"It was some kind of miracle then." It seemed to be the only explanation, as vague as it was.

"We can ask David when he gets here. Maybe he'll have an idea."

"You never told me why he wants to talk to me." Jay

hoped she'd open up and tell him what to expect, so there would be no surprises.

"This place is super-secret. It's the rules. Everyone has to report to him before coming here."

"Before?" Jay lifted his brow. "But I'm already here."

"You're an exception." She smiled, and Jay wondered why. Before he could ask, she continued, "The Grays know nothing about this place. Only a handful of Units do. It's called, Underneath the Underground or UU. Some call it, the Double U."

"Oh, so that's what that Kahl dude meant. Why do the Units need a secret place?"

"The Grays don't give the Units much freedom. We're like second-class citizens. We do all the labor, and they treat us like animals. It's gone on too long and we just want equality. This place gives us somewhere to go where we can be ourselves, without fear."

"Still don't get how I'm involved."

"I guess you're not, really. Let's wait for David and he can answer your questions." She continued shifted in her seat, wiggling and rubbing against the back of the chair in an attempt to scratch an itch.

So many questions swam around in Jay's brain. This David guy was taking forever, and Jay couldn't hold his tongue. "How do you keep the Grays from finding out about the Double U?"

"Grays don't like tight, enclosed spaces and refuse to go in them. That's why we've chosen to go this far down through narrow passageways. Oh, and Grays hate bugs. So, we have the trap."

"You told me before that Units and Grays have always

been here. What does that mean?" Jay asked, remembering.

"Just that, Jay. You all evolved out there." She pointed up. "We evolved in here. We're underground people."

"Then why the alien-looking dudes? Why do they look like that?"

"The *Grays* evolved that way," she stressed the word. "Whatever you read in those books, it's completely wrong. Outsiders made up stuff. Someone saw a Gray and didn't know what to make of it, so they came up with some crazy stories about creatures from the stars. But they're just stories. That's all they are."

"You should read the books. There's a ton of people who say they've seen Grays. They really believe they're aliens from outer space." All this time they've lived underground? It was difficult to swallow.

"Like I mentioned, outsiders have come up with lots of ridiculous things. I'm telling you, they aren't true. I don't need to read a book to know that."

"How can you be so sure?"

"Jay, there are hundreds of thousands of tunnels and rooms throughout the mountain area which go for hundreds of thousands of miles. Do you think all of that was built in a day? The Underground has been around for thousands of years. Generations of Grays and Units have lived here. Ancient drawings are on the cave walls that show our history. We've been here as long as you've been up there."

She had a good point. It was something he couldn't refute. Still, some things didn't fit. "Why doesn't anyone above ground know about it then?" Jay scratched ferociously at his arm, the bright red bites starting to swell. "And that the Grays live here?"

"The Grays don't like sunlight. It damages their skin, so they stay away from it most of the time. It's rare any of them would venture outside of the Underground for any length of time. And they've been careful to hide our home. What do you think would happen if people up there found out we live down here? Especially if they discovered the Grays?"

Jay considered it, and the scenario wasn't pretty. Capture and experimentation came to mind.

"You see?" Nina responded, noticing his expression. "Of course, the outsiders try to find an explanation for the Grays. They're afraid of what they don't understand."

That did make sense. What better explanation could you come up with than aliens from space? He probably would have thought the same. "What about Units? What about you?"

Nina brushed her hair away from her eyes. "We're distant cousins to the Grays. We're alike in some ways. The sunlight doesn't bother us as much. But we're told we can't live above ground because there can be side effects for us if we're outside too long."

"Like what?"

"They say the atmosphere will give us horrible diseases and the sun will age us quickly and kill us over time."

Jay wondered if it was all government propaganda, similar to the tactics governments above the earth's surface use to keep the masses under their control. "It doesn't seem like anything's happened to you." Dad always said to never trust the government. Then again, Dad didn't trust anyone. "Maybe the Grays are lying."

Nina tightened her lips and moved them to the side. "David says that, too. I used to believe everything they told us. Not as much anymore."

"It's so weird they've kept this place secret for so long. I mean, I found it." He shrugged a shoulder.

"That was my fault." she bowed her head. "I got careless. I wasn't thinking." She took a deep breath and spoke while exhaling. "I could get my outside access taken away for that."

"Your what?"

Nina shooed it off. "Never mind. We were going to bring you down here anyway. The time just got moved up a little. The real reason I brought you here is so we could ask you for a favor."

"A favor?" Jay raised his eyebrows. He couldn't imagine what they would want from him. "What favor?" he asked, not sure he wanted to hear the answer. "And why do you keep saying 'we'?"

"First, I should start out explaining how things work around here so you understand. Grays believe themselves to be evolved beings. They're much more intelligent than Units. They say they know what's best for us because Units brains aren't as developed.

"All the Units have four letters in their name and the Grays have three. The numbers identify us. So, my full name is N-I-N-A dash 22898, like that."

"Oh, I see. That's why that guy, Kahl, thought I spelled my name J-A-Y- E."

"Right. If you tell anyone your name is, J-A-Y, they'd think you're a Gray in disguise." She stared at him as if he should know what that meant, receiving an unsure nod in return. "That would not be good."

"Of course not." Jay frowned, wishing she'd elaborate.

"Grays can't find out about this place. None of them. You can't trust Grays." She cocked her head and tilted her forehead toward him. "You'll be okay as long as you remember that. Never trust a Gray."

"Okay, but how the heck could I be a Gray?"

"They've got disguises to look like Units."

"Really?' He smirked and released a quiet laugh. "They must be amazing disguises."

"They are. Grays would be too nervous to come down this far underground anyway, but that's not the point. Kahl would've been suspicious if you'd told him your name has three letters. David hasn't told him you're here yet."

Jay shook his head, still confused at how a disguise could be so realistic that you'd believe one of those creepy Gray things was human. "Why would David tell Kahl about me?"

"I'll explain. But I gotta finish this part first." Nina scratched a bump her cheek, fidgeting, looking uncomfortable. "Grays don't really have emotions outside of anger. They hate that Units have emotions. It drives them crazy. Also, if a Gray or a Unit shows sickness or gets too old, they destroy them. Kill and burn."

"Kill and burn?" Jay's face tightened.

"They see age as weakness."

These Grays were even worse than he thought. "They're psychopaths." He thought of serial killers. That's exactly what these things were. It made him nauseous. "What do they consider old?"

"Whatever they determine. And it changes."

"Wow. Why would they do that?"

"It's the way things are. We can't do anything about it. If you say something or look into someone who disappeared, you might disappear too. Believe me, it's happened."

"That's messed up."

"Now you see why the Units must be freed."

Jay kept his gaze straight ahead, unsure of what to say. This whole thing was crazy, like right out of a movie.

"It's been told both races evolved in separate places—a Unit tribe underground to the south and the Grays to the north." She motioned to one side, then the other, as if pointing out opposite ends of a map. "The two races found each other as they both grew and migrated together."

"That sucks for the Units."

"Yeah." Nina forced a small smile as Jay watched her, clearly anxious for more. "David knows a lot more of the history than I do."

"Wait." Jay realized David's name didn't follow the rules. "David has more than four letters."

"His full name is DVID–9334 but we pronounce his name 'David'."

"Oh. It's like license plates. There're unlimited combinations."

Nina skewed her mouth to the left with a frown.

Jay ignored her confusion, deciding to keep asking questions as long as he was able before David came in. "What does David do as the leader?"

"Lots of things."

"Like what?"

"David helps screen the Units. We can't be too careful. Some Units have been brainwashed to side with the Grays against their own people. David trusts you, though. I told him all about you. He knows pretty much everything I know." Jay's face grew hot, remembering the comment he'd made regarding Lydia and the kiss, and wondered if she'd told him. "David's like a dad to me, or a big brother. He also leads and trains the Unit army. He gives me my Power Lessons. He's been giving me extra ones in secret because of what I'm really training for."

"What are you really training for?"

Nina clamped her lips tight.

"Let me guess," Jay responded, tilting his chin down. "David will tell me, right?"

She smiled. "Don't worry, Jay. It'll be fine."

Jay blew a raspberry. "That's what you said about the bugs."

"You are fine, aren't you?"

"Barely." Jay let out a nervous chuckle. "What are Power Lessons, anyway?"

"I'm not very good at explaining things." Nina ran her hand through her long, messy hair anxiously as she collected her thoughts. "All right, I'm a spy." She put her small hand on her chest as she talked. At the end of the sentence, her voice went up high, making her sound more like a little girl.

This made Jay grin.

"What?" Her brow tightened slightly.

His thoughts went to James Bond. "You don't look much like a spy."

She placed a fist on her hip. "Yeah? How many spies have you talked to?"

"Well..."

"Exactly. Now be quiet and listen."

Jay laughed softly, but she paid him no attention. Maybe "spy" meant something else in the Underground.

"We have our own government down here. There's a queen who's a Unit, and a Gray king. The king is above everyone and everything. Some Units believe the queen is dead, even though we've been told by the king that she rules secretly because she doesn't want to be seen in public anymore. Neither of which are true. I'll tell you how I know in a minute."

She took a breath before continuing. "The government officials are Grays. When we had a queen, they supposedly would help her rule, although she supposedly had the final say over them."

"You said supposedly twice."

"That's 'cause David says it's never been true. He says the queen has always been just a figurehead to appease the Units."

"So, the queen never had power?"

"Not in the Stoneburrow government. That's what David says. It's all a scam." She pointed to her head. "A trick of the mind. Anyway, one or two of the officials represent each city, depending on how large it is. My city is called, Majestic."

"I remember seeing that by the entrance. It's a cool name."

"Next on the chain of command after the queen and the officials are the authorities. Their job is to keep order among the Units. Yag is one. The Gray that stopped you in the Great Room? Then come the other workers, like trainers and spies, and there're three different levels of spies. Spies-in-Training, Underground Spies, and Superior Spies." She held up a finger for each as she recited them. "I am a Superior Spy and I'm the youngest ever to reach that level. I don't have parents. David took me in when I was a kid. He's been training me my whole life. He calls my training, Power Lessons, because they are special —different from normal government issued training."

Jay cleared his throat. Nina was talking a mile a minute, and it was the only way he could squeeze a word in edge wise. "What happened to your parents?"

"I was told my father died before I was born, and my mother died at my birth."

"Doesn't sound like you believe that."

"I'm not sure if I do or not. But it's not unusual for kids not to have parents down here."

"What? Why?"

"It just isn't." She sighed. "It's just the way it is."

Jay suddenly understood. "Kill and burn?"

Nina shrugged, a hint of sadness on her face. "Anyway, to be a Superior Spy, the highest level of spy, you have to be great at it, but you also have to prove yourself worthy of the title. That could be anything from ratting someone out who's doing something against the government, capturing an escaped criminal, or anything brave to save someone in Stoneburrow."

"So, what did you do?"

"I'll answer that soon."

Jay leaned his elbow on the arm of the chair and rested his head on his palm. He curled his fingers on his cheek, trying to absorb everything she was saying, although with so much information, his brain felt like it might explode. Plus, her fast talking was making his head spin. He wondered if he had ever heard anyone talk so much or so fast in his life.

"I am good at defusing traps," she continued. "That's like my specialty, and these tunnels are full of them. A lot of times, David and the others will use me for that. Like if they want to get through a tunnel, usually I can find a way through the trap. The only one I haven't been able to crack is the bug one outside the door. David says it's a good trap because it keeps the ones that don't belong here away. It only goes off when headed to the Double U through that tunnel, not when you leave in the same direction. We try to avoid going that way. Usually we can."

"How are these traps here, anyway? I mean, they are magical, aren't they? Who put them there?"

"David says the queen created them. He says the new traps show she's still alive."

All this magic stuff was confusing to Jay. "How does she create them? Is she a witch?"

"A witch? No. She has powers though."

"What kind of powers?"

"Jay, I've got to tell you something before David gets here. Please, let me finish."

"Fine. It's just strange." He plopped the weight of his head back on his hand, wondering how much longer she would go on.

"I know. But listen. About six months ago, I found a tunnel I had never been through before. I noticed it had traps, so I decided it was the perfect opportunity to practice my trap skills. The government officials had the queen create traps in the tunnels where they don't want anyone to go, and in the ones leading to the outside. That made me curious too."

"Because they want to keep people inside." It was becoming clearer to Jay the longer she talked.

"Well, yeah. I guess that's part of it. So, this tunnel I found went far away from the other tunnels," Nina continued. "Which scared me, but I really felt I should keep going, so I did. I saw a flicker of yellow light coming from beyond the cave wall. I crept into the room to find an area with bars on it. It was a jail cell.

"Our jail area is in a different place in Stoneburrow, and the prisoners are all together. But this cell was by itself. A small lamp was burning on a table outside the bars, and the flickering light made the whole room feel mysterious and creepy. It was as if I was in a dream. When I got closer, I could see a lady sitting in the very middle of the cell. I swear, she didn't look real. She looked like a corpse or a life-size doll or something.

"She was bent over and quietly crying. When she sensed me there, she lifted her head. Her face looked old and tired, and her eyes were empty and sad. She kind of stared at me with a blank look, like she didn't really believe I was there. I said hi to her, and she returned my greeting in a dry, cracked voice.

"I was afraid because I didn't know who she was, but I didn't sense any kind of danger. I was more nervous that someone would catch me there than anything. But I sat down in front of the bars anyway. I could've reached in and touched her if I wanted to. Being near the woman comforted me in a way. For some reason, I never wanted to leave her.

""What are you doing in here?' I asked her, and she

said, 'I'm a prisoner.' 'What have you done to get arrested?' I asked. 'I ran away,' she said. I asked her who she was, and she told me. She said she was the queen."

"The queen? You met the queen?" Jay leaned forward in his chair, his hands in fists between his knees, holding on to her every word.

"Yes, and I don't know if she's still alive or dead. In my heart, I believe she's alive. So does David." Nina gazed deeply into Jay's eyes, a glow of passion in her own. "I want to free her," she declared urgently. "We want to," she corrected herself. "She doesn't deserve to be there."

"Why is she?"

"Her desire to be free. She ran off to live on the outside. They captured her and brought her back."

"I thought you said she was ruling in secret."

"That's what we've always been told. After discovering her locked up, I realized that wasn't true. The truth is, she escaped and lived above ground for years before they found her and put her in the cell. David estimates that she'd been imprisoned for about eleven years when I found her."

"The environment didn't destroy her, like the Grays say it will," Jay realized, and Nina nodded. "So, what does all this got to do with me?"

"We need to save her."

"I got that. But—"

"We need help."

"From me? What can *I* do?" Did she really believe he could find and free their queen in an underground world he never knew existed until today?

"Did he say yes?" a deep male voice drifted to them from just inside the curtain. Both of them jumped at the sound. It came from the man with the black, hollow-looking eyes. He wore clothes similar to Jay's, though his fit him perfectly. He was asking Nina, holding out a glass of yellowish liquid in each hand, but his gaze stayed on Jay. More than ever, something about him felt familiar. "Is he going to help us?"

As Jay bit into his lower lip, he wondered what in the world he had gotten himself into.

27

THE QUEEN

"Well?" David said. Nina didn't answer for a few seconds, but the timeframe seemed so much longer in the silence of the room.

"I haven't gotten to that part."

"I see." David set the two drinks on a desk, one in front of each of them. Both said thank you in unison, Jay's voice more of a background noise. Jay eyed the yellow liquid in the glass with suspicion. He had seen enough movies to know not to drink anything a strange person with black, hollow-looking eyes would give you.

David pulled out a tube of something from his pocket and extended it to Nina. "Thank the queen below," she said. "Can you rub it on my back?"

He squeezed some onto his fingers before passing the tube to Jay. After rubbing the ointment on a very grateful Nina's back, he wiped the remains on the legs of his jeans. "Mind if I sit?"

Jay said nothing, shrugging to reflect he didn't care,

although he wasn't totally sure. Something about the man made him uncomfortable. Yet, his demeanor and his voice commanded a presence—appearing that he could bring a crowd to attention with just a word. Jay could see why this group would choose him to lead.

Nina grinned. "Grab a seat." David still wasn't looking at her and seemed to direct the question to Jay. Jay wished he would turn his attention toward Nina and take those creepy eyes off him for a little while.

David pulled up a chair, sitting on it backwards, one knee pointed in Jay's direction and the other in Nina's, his large, pale hands resting on the backrest. His legs were long and thin in his tight black pants, and he wore black boots with a heavy tread on the sole. He appeared to be in his mid-twenties, had dark hair and a good-looking face. Two lines trailed from the sides of his nose down to the corners of his thin lips with one permanent crease between his eyebrows, revealing that the guy probably both smiled and frowned a lot.

"That ointment help?" he asked Jay, who nodded without a sound. "How are you both doing after almost becoming bug food? You okay?"

Nina nodded with lips tight. "Just itchy. But much better now."

"Good. Finish talking. Pretend I'm not here," David told them. That was a lot easier said than done, especially for Jay, who felt very intimidated.

"Do you want to tell him?" Nina spoke in a high-pitched voice, her wide, innocent eyes fixed on David.

"Sure. I'll explain the gist of it then you can take it from there. Sound good?" David's tone was comforting, like he was talking to his daughter. Jay understood why Nina trusted him, although he wasn't sure he himself ever would. David turned back to Jay, changing his voice and demeanor to all business. "Listen. We believe the queen is alive and imprisoned below, even further down than we are now. We wish to free her."

"Why?" Jay asked.

David's forehead wrinkled, the vertical crease between his eyes intensifying. Jay began to think he wasn't going to answer and lowered his eyes, unable to keep them locked with David's a moment longer.

But he did. "There're several reasons. First, the Grays used her like a pawn. They tried to make everyone think she ruled Stoneburrow to appease the Units. But all of us in the Double U know that's a load of crap." He leaned forward. "They number us, you know. The number after our name? They number the Grays and the Units."

Jay nodded with a tight brow, remembering the license plate method the Grays used to name everyone and wondering where David was going with this.

"The Units are growing in number and that makes the Grays nervous. They're afraid of an uprising." He studied Jay with an intense frown, causing him to lower his gaze again to the floor, feeling uneasy. "Tell me, Jay." Jay raised his head and cocked it in question. "What's the difference between putting an equal number of Units and Grays in power over the community," he put his hands vertically parallel to each other on the right side of him, then switched them over to the left, "and putting a Unit queen in power over everyone?"

Jay shrugged.

"I'll tell you. The first way, the Grays lose their power

base. The second way, they satisfy the Units by having them believe the Unit queen is ruling, while behind the scenes manipulating her into doing whatever the heck they want her to do."

"I guess that makes sense."

"Yes. And the king is an elderly Gray we rarely see." He leaned in and glared at Jay. "I've only seen him a few times and he's really old—like older than this cave floor. It's weird because you never find a Gray that old in the Underground."

Jay turned to Nina in time to see her mouth the words, "Kill and burn."

"Right," Jay said, remembering.

David continued. "Before the queen disappeared, the old king would call all the shots, and the queen would announce them as if they were her ideas. Trust me, she was not happy about that."

"I wouldn't think so." Jay thought about it a moment. "She had to marry an old Gray?"

"No. It's not a marriage. Trust me, a Gray has no interest in a Unit no matter how beautiful. He only wanted to use her." David leaned back a bit, shaking his head in sympathy. "She wasn't one to be harnessed, the queen. They underestimated her. She escaped, and the Grays tried to cover it up. Instead, the king announced she would rule in secret. After they captured her, they continued the lie." David slapped his hands on the backrest, which made Jay jump in his skin. "It can't go on. We have to save her."

"Okay." Jay was still unsure why they kept saying "we" and what he had to do with it. Meanwhile, David stared at him, as if Jay would provide some sort of solution. "So, what does all this have to do with me?" he finally asked, unable to take the silence anymore. What did they think he could contribute? This was a huge, dangerous problem in their world, and he was just a kid from the outside.

"You're strong."

Jay repressed the urge to laugh. "Me?"

David nodded.

"You have the wrong idea. I'm not strong. I come from a long line of wimps."

David's brow furrowed, and a stern look overtook his face. He stuck out his finger. "No, you do not." When Jay jerked his head back, puzzled, David lowered his hand and composed himself. Then, with the same hand, he reached up to Jay's throat. Before Jay could retract, he grasped the ring hanging on his necklace in his fingers. "You are strong." He showed Jay the ring as if he might be unaware of its existence. "You're stronger than you realize, and with my training, you'll see it too." He let loose of the ring, and it thumped lightly on Jay's skinny chest.

Jay grabbed the ring in his own fist as he had done many times when he felt frightened. "Training?" David's words were starting to make him nervous, and he had no intention of participating in any kind of war training.

"And David," Nina interrupted, capturing his attention. "When we were outside the door, the bugs covered me and when Jay touched me, they flew off in flames."

"Really?" David straightened up, sitting on the edge of his seat.

"Yes, but I had nothing to do with that," Jay insisted.

David peered at him sideways. "Are you sure?"

"Of course. I...I would know if I'd done something like that. I wouldn't even know how to."

"Well, tell me what happened exactly." David leaned back, crossing his muscular arms.

"That's all that happened." Jay shrugged. "The bugs covered her and then they flew off and burst into flames."

"Hmm." David looked off to the side in thought.

Nina sat up straight. "All I know is I was buried in bugs, then there was this bright red light, and suddenly they weren't on me anymore. It had to have been Jay. No one else was around."

David's eyes grew wide, revealing more of the white around his dark irises. "A red light?"

"Yes," Nina replied. They both turned their focus on Jay.

Jay looked from Nina to David and back again. "I don't know what you're suggesting, but I can't perform magic." He laughed. "I'm not Harry Potter." Couldn't they hear how ridiculous they sounded?

"Who?" David frowned as they continued to study him. Nina bit her lip.

"Never mind." Jay kept forgetting that he was speaking to people that literally had been living in a hole in the ground. "For real. Be serious."

Nina and David exchanged a glance as if they shared a secret.

"What?" Jay asked Nina, exasperated. When he turned back to David, it hit him out of nowhere. "Wait, I have seen you before." He pointed to him, much like David had done only seconds before, his memory rekindling. "I've seen you a few times when I walked to school, before Nina came around."

"Yes, you did." David's voice was soothing and calm. "After I found you, Nina took over for me."

"Found me?" Jay looked back and forth between David and Nina. "Why were you following me? And what does my ring have to do with all this?" His eyes found Nina's who seemed to have trouble maintaining eye contact. "How did you know I lost it the day I followed you into the tunnel? Please, someone, tell me what's going on."

David turned to Nina and raised his thick eyebrows. "I guess this is where you come in, Nina."

She nodded. "Okay, well, um. That day, the one when I stumbled upon the queen in the jail cell? She explained to me about her escape and capture. I asked her other questions, but she stopped answering me. She would say things unrelated like, 'You're so pretty.' And 'I had children.' Stuff like that. She slurred her words like she was all drugged up or something.

"Then, she sat up, like she just realized I was there. 'Do something for me,' she said. I agreed and asked her what she wanted. 'Please check on my family. Watch them, please.' She told me they were living on the outside. She kept saying, 'Make sure they're okay.' I wasn't a Supreme Spy yet, and I explained that to her. I told her I was skilled, but had done nothing to prove myself, so for me to go above ground was impossible. The government would never give me that much freedom.

"She remained quiet and still for a while and wouldn't answer any of my questions. I decided I would leave, thinking something had happened to her or she'd lost her mind, until she started talking again. She noticed the blade in my belt and told me to set her free and she would show me how I could prove myself.

"I thought it must be a trick, but she insisted that her plan would work. She told me not to worry about getting caught, that the guards only came once in the morning to feed her a small meal and that was it. The rest of the time, she was in isolation, and it had been that way for years.

"She gave me instructions. Once I let her go, I was to call the authorities and tell them she'd escaped. This would demonstrate myself worthy and I would be promoted as Supreme Spy. I asked her if she was afraid of being punished for trying to escape or of being tortured again, and she insisted that she wasn't. She said she didn't care what happened to her. All she cared about was her family. She said, 'My life is over anyway. Every day, I pray for death and if it comes to me as punishment, it will be no less than a reward to my soul.' I will never forget that. The look in her tired eyes told me all I needed to know. That's what convinced me.

"David taught me how to pick locks. I'm pretty good at it and got her jail cell open in about two minutes. She was so relieved that she hugged me and said something strange. She whispered, 'I knew you would come.'"

"What did that mean?" Jay wondered aloud.

With sadness in her eyes, Nina replied, "I'm not exactly sure."

Jay tilted his head. "Did they catch her?"

"Yes, they did. As soon as she let go of me, she grabbed my blade and took off down the tunnels faster than I would've imagined she could, considering she'd been sitting still for so many years. She made fresh tunnels with my blade. It was amazing, like the earth just parted for her." Nina put her hands together and pulled them apart to illustrate. "The rocks literally jumped out of her way, and a red light blinked with every slash.

"When I yelled for her to stop, she screamed back, 'I have to see it.' I didn't know what she meant. At the time, I was sure she had tricked me. So, I contacted the authorities through my CND, my Communication and Navigation Device, though I really didn't want to.

"I chased after her and was somehow able to keep up the entire time. Then she stopped. From a distance, I heard the authorities approaching. She returned my blade and grabbed my CND, which I now have attached to the back of my dog collar." Nina pulled the collar from her pocket and flipped it over, revealing a small, black rectangular device with tiny buttons. "She pressed the buttons, programming it I guess, and then another red light flashed. She handed the CND back to me. When I asked what she'd done, she told me, 'I set it so you can locate my family. It's set to my ring. When you find it, you will find them. I had a husband and a child.'"

Nina swallowed hard. "Because it took a while for me to get my Supreme Spy status and be allowed to go on the outside, David tracked down the ring for me and when he did, he found..."

Jay rubbed the ring on the chain around his neck with his fingers, feeling grief in his heart and a lump in his throat. "Me," he finished for her.

Nina smiled and nodded. "Yes."

"So, you're telling me the queen..." Jay had trouble saying the words. How could they be right? How could what they were suggesting be true? Mom had died in a fire. Dad and Aunt Vicki had said so. He looked at them, silently pleading, waiting for them to say something, anything that would contradict what they seemed to be trying to tell him. But that was not to be.

"Yes, Jay," David said in a kind voice, as if he were talking to a mental patient that could snap at any moment. "The queen is your mother."

28

THE NEED FOR THE BOY

The two men sat across from each other, eyes locked, elbows on the table. It looked less like a friendly chat and more like a negotiation between two opponents on rival teams—no matter how strongly Kahl and David might deny it. The tall one on one side and the short, stocky one on the other seemed caught in a game that required more strategy than either would admit.

"We seem to be wasting our time here. Why do we need this boy?" Kahl asked after Jay and Nina had left the Double U and David filled him in on their conversation. "You're telling me that kid is the queen's child?"

"Yes. And I just told you why. He's part of the prophecy. Once we get this team together, our plan will come together, and we'll regain power."

"Power that never existed cannot be regained," Kahl assured him, taking a casual drink from his cup.

David rolled his eyes, tired of Kahl's repetitive arguments. "Kahl, you know what I mean. It's time for a change. The queen should rule—I mean really rule, not just serve as a figurehead. It is only then that the Units will finally be free."

"I'm not sure that will matter. Or if it's even possible. But that's an argument for a different time. We're uncertain the queen is even alive. Some say she isn't. Some say she is and is ruling in secret."

"Yeah," David huffed. "That comes from the Grays, and you know it's a complete lie. They wouldn't allow her to make any real decisions."

"And some say she ran off, was captured and killed. That's my bet. If she's not ruling, what reason would the Grays have for sustaining her? All logic says she's dead, my friend."

Nothing Kahl could say would deter him from what he knew to be the truth. "I saw her."

"You saw her. Past tense, not present."

"But it was only seven months ago!" David slammed his fist on the hard surface of the table. "She told me to build this army, and I told her I would. She had one of Makk's stones."

"Ah, the stone the half-Gray creature found. The Paragon?"

"Yes."

"I always assumed the Paragon was legend, as most people do, created by Units desperate for a miracle. You sure it's not?"

"No, I knew Makk." It had been many years since David was told his childhood friend was dead, and he still missed him. "I've seen the stone he found and have witnessed its power."

"It's impossible." Kahl frowned. "You said the boy, Jay, has the queen's Paragon. She can't possibly have it if it's around the boy's neck."

"She has another piece. Remember three were cut from it. This one has meshed with her somehow."

"How do you mean?" Kahl peered at him from the sides of his eyes.

"She has a Paragon in her body," David told him. "She says Makk put it there, although it's impossible. Makk has been dead for years, so I don't know how she got it. I suppose being alone for so long has truly made her delusional and perhaps mad. Is it possible her connection to the Paragon is so strong she drew it to herself?"

Kahl frowned, running his fingers through his thinning hair. "Maybe. And yet, are you sure this Makk is dead? Have you ever tried to find him?"

"No, shamefully I haven't. But others have."

"Seems there're a lot of places to hide in the tunnel system."

"If the queen truly does have Makk's Paragon, I'm sure he's dead." Makk was unable to feel much, but he loved that Paragon. David thought the stone might have opened up his ability to have some emotions, and the only thing he cared about more than that rock was the queen herself. "He would have never parted with it. Not to mention, I received word of his death on good authority."

"But doesn't it stand to reason, my friend," Kahl shifted in his seat, "if she had this Paragon, wouldn't she have long since freed herself?"

"You miss the point. She wants freedom for the Units as much as I do. As much as we all do. She's waiting for the right time for the prophecy to be revealed. Also, after

Nina found her, she believes her husband and her son are dead which most assuredly has drained her of hope."

"Didn't you tell her you've been in contact with Vicki and Jay is fine?"

David bowed his head. "No. She still thinks they both died in the fire."

Kahl blew air out of his puckered lips. "Poor thing."

David met Kahl's eyes and with all sincerity said, "It's for the best."

"How so?"

"If she knew her son was alive, she might be tempted to leave again. Think of the first time and what she did to get to him. Wherever she is now, we need her to remain there until the war begins."

"That we do."

"Even if I did want to tell her, just to ease her pain, it's impossible now. We don't know where she is since they've relocated her, do we?"

Kahl shook his head, directing his gaze to the table-top. "Or killed her."

"Please don't say that."

"It is a possibility. If she is alive, and she does truly believe her family is dead, why wouldn't she just escape?"

"I'm sure they are threatening her with other things. Maybe the death of other people in her life."

"Like who?"

"Others she knows in the Underground. Vicki, for one." He bit the inside of his cheek and studied his hands on the tabletop. "And me."

"You?" Kahl tightened his lips. "Why you?"

"The king is aware of my past."

"It all seems illogical."

"It isn't. They haven't figured out how she uses the Paragon to create the miracles she does. They need that information." David always thought there was something more sinister lurking when it came to the queen's imprisonment. "And maybe there's something they want her to do with it."

"I don't doubt the Grays are up to something," Kahl uttered, and David was glad they finally agreed on something. "But it's been months since you've seen her and she could very well be dead, as has been rumored. Perhaps they figured out how to use the Paragon and ran out of use for her."

David shook his head. "No. They lied about her death before. They're lying now."

"Maybe. But even so, why shouldn't you and I rule? We are more than capable."

"No." David would never take over the queen's position. He wasn't worthy of it. "The queen. It must be the queen. She has superior powers, not me, not you." David rubbed his cheeks with both hands, then traveled to his eyes. Grunting, he grabbed the armrests of his chair and sat up straight. "We're getting nowhere with this. We need to finalize a plan."

"But the boy... I'm not sure it's a good idea." Kahl raised his eyebrows in concern. "Maybe it's not the right time."

"I'm sorry you feel that way, but I'm following my instincts on this. I've already discussed it with Nina."

Kahl leaned over the table. "With Nina? You consulted with Nina? A little girl? Before me? And I'm only hearing of this now?" He leaned back into his chair and crossed his arms. "I'm getting the feeling I'm not your second in line after all."

"Don't be crazy."

"How long have you two been conspiring with the queen's spawn on the outside?" He threw his hand upward.

"I told you. I only met him today. Vicki has been protecting him from me. From everyone. She's bound and determined not to let anything happen to him. But he's part of this prophecy, and those are the risks. Whether she likes it or not."

"A little girl," Kahl shook his head, clearly disheartened. "You consult her before me."

David closed his eyes in frustration. "I'm telling you now." Why must he be so difficult? Why must he question everything? His skepticism made it burdensome to talk to him. If he only had more faith.

"Snopes, David. You seem to have this all under control. Are we still on the same team? Or have you flipped?"

"Kahl, don't say things like that. We can't move forward without you." David smiled at him, trying his best to be reassuring. "Besides, I don't tell Nina everything, I promise you. I can't."

"I would hope not. And this brings us to the prophecy."

David sighed, knowing what was coming.

"We don't know the prediction from the old Unit to be factual."

"You doubt so much, Kahl. You need to believe." Kahl was cunning. He was, after all, a servant to the Gray's government, as David was himself. Although, in actuality, they were both aligned in secret to defeat the Grays and bring the Units into power. He knew he could trust Kahl. But there was one thing Kahl lacked. He couldn't be led easily. And David was not a follower. "You know all of this. The queen told me exactly how to get the prophecy. I saved that old lady's life because of her."

"Old Mary. Snopes, she was old."

"She's still alive, I believe. Although I've not seen her in years."

"That female was a little off her rock, if you ask me."

"Yet known to be correct in her predictions of the future." David remembered Mary well. She was like a mother to Tara. She wasn't crazy, despite Kahl's opinion of her. The woman was smarter than anyone David had ever met.

"Guess that's why the Grays let her live so long." It was an interesting observation. They permitted no one to live as old as she. Kill and burn. The Grays did this as Units aged or if they got sick. "And also, why they harbored her away at the end. But I still don't know if we should put all our hope into her prophecy. It seems odd."

"Maybe. But when I found Mary, she told me she had been expecting me. She pointed to her head and said, 'I saw you talking to the queen.' Just before I left her, she recited the prophecy to me."

Kahl leaned forward. "You confess yourself you may not remember it all accurately."

"There was no time to memorize it. But my memory is good. She was smart to write in poetry form to make it easier. And I promise you, it is the real thing. You know she has the gift."

"Okay, fine." Kahl took a long drink and wiped his mouth with the back of his hand. "Say I believe in this prophecy. And, let's say, I even trust that you remember it perfectly. How will we know when it's time to act?"

"Once we assemble all five, I will lead the fight." David had every confidence it would work. The fulfillment of the prophecy would free them all and finally put the Units in control. They would no longer be slaves, trapped underground, but free to do as they pleased. Old Mary believed, the queen believed, and he believed. If only Kahl had as much faith. It was almost as if he didn't want to be free.

"And what if you aren't the leader according to the prediction?" Kahl said, crossing his arms to his chest once more.

"I am," David insisted, tilting his head back. "We've discussed this. Remember, there are five laid out in the prophecy." He used his fingers to count them. "The Trap Tricker, that's Nina. The Sharp Shooter, that's you because you can hit darn near anything with a knife. The Royal One, of course, that's the queen who is also the Healer. And the Swordsman who is fast and good with a sword, we are assuming to be Jay. Then there's the Decipherer, which is me because I have the prediction. And, it says, the young at heart will lead them."

"Well, there you go." Kahl threw both hands up.

"What?"

"You're not that young. I mean, obviously you aren't younger than the rest of us."

"That's not what is says, Kahl. It says young at heart, and that is obviously me." David placed his hand on his chest with full confidence.

"Originally you told me it said, youngest heart. There's a difference."

David's patience was running thin. "Kahl, please. You need to have faith in me. I'm the one with the deciphering skills."

"We don't know that's true either," Kahl uttered under his breath as he took another sip.

"What was that?"

"Nothing. I said nothing." Kahl cleared his throat as David studied him with suspicion. "Besides, this boy hasn't agreed to join us."

Maybe Kahl was unsure, but David had no doubt in his mind. "He will. I'm not worried about it. Believe in something for once in your miserable life. It will work out, I'm telling you."

"If you say so."

"Vicki isn't happy about it though," David pursed his lips.

"Oh, yeah?" Kahl perked up a bit, curious. "How is ole' Vicki, anyway?"

"She's fine. Mad at me, but fine." David played with the rim of his cup, distracted with worry about making Vicki upset. Despite what she believed, he didn't want that. "She wants me to leave Jay out of it."

"Perhaps she's right."

"No, Kahl. She is not. She's not right at all. Without him, the prophecy can't happen." It still baffled him why Kahl didn't understand this. "Besides, Jay has the same power as the queen. What more proof do you need?"

Kahl sat up with a frown. "He does, does he?"

"Nina saw it herself. When the bugs flew off her, she swears she saw a red light."

"The infamous red light. Maybe there is something to this boy."

"See." David threw his hands up and sat back in his chair, glad his words were finally sinking in.

"But that still doesn't mean he's in the prophecy. It speaks nothing about the queen's child."

"Oh, Kahl. How you doubt, just like Vicki."

Kahl started to take another drink before noticing his cup was empty and set it down. "I've never even met this, Vicki. For all I know she doesn't exist."

David made a sound through his teeth. "What? Now I'm lying about Vicki?" Was there anything Kahl believed? How could he have chosen someone to work with on such an important mission who seemed to believe in absolutely nothing? He was thankful for Nina. It shouldn't be a mystery why he confided in her so much. She had faith in him one hundred percent, which said a lot about her loyalty.

"No, I'm not saying that. It's just odd you haven't intro-duced me." He looked deep in thought. "You still giving her those pills?"

"Yeah, I have to. She needs them to survive on the outside." Most of Vicki's insides were Gray and, like the Grays, her lungs had trouble transferring oxygen to her blood. The Grays developed a solution in pill form, which David was forced to steal for her. He wasn't sure if he could continue doing so once the battle began. He couldn't think that far ahead and supposed he'd take it one day at a time.

"She still living in the same place?"

"Same as last we talked, yes. She has her home hidden from the Grays with the Paragon."

"Ah, well, the Paragon didn't do the queen much good. Did it?" Kahl twirled his empty glass around and around on the table with one hand.

"Not once the Grays figured out where she was. No, it didn't. Caught right outside the circle. Just heart-breaking."

"Vicki still healing, I suppose?"

"Yes. Working with animals," David answered with a nod. Vicki had grown amazingly powerful with the Paragon. He only wished she'd join forces with them. That power would be extremely valuable. But she was too emotionally invested, and he couldn't trust her to make the tough decisions when it became necessary.

"Hmm."

"You know," David sat up in his chair, "the last thing Old Mary suggested was to watch for spies. I wonder what that could mean."

"I'm sure it means to be on your guard and watch for Gray spies. They do have spies. That's not surprising."

"Right, but it makes you wonder why she specifically mentioned it. She must have sensed something."

"I suppose we'll see."

"I don't want to just wait and see." David smacked the armrest with his fist. "We must keep our eyes wide open and be alert at all times. Can you spot a spy?"

Kahl looked beyond David to the wall, nodding his head once. "From a mile away, brother. From a mile away."

"Great. Keep on your toes. Don't draw any attention."

"Of course not."

"I owe you a lot, Kahl. I trust you with my life. If not

for you, I would have been destroyed by the Grays long ago. I hope you know you can trust me as well." He flashed him a crooked smile.

Kahl nodded again but said nothing.

29

THE HOUSE

Jay straightened the brim of his cap as he and Nina returned down the tunnel where the bugs had nearly devoured them an hour earlier. All the critters were gone, even the dead ones, as if they never existed at all. Although amazed, he was too upset to ask Nina where they'd gone. Were they created out of thin air by magic or were they lurking behind the cave walls waiting to be summoned?

David stayed behind in the Double U, saying it would be too dangerous for all three of them to be seen together walking through the tunnels. The fact that the bug trap wouldn't be tripped leaving the UU, only when headed toward it, was reassuring. He was in no mood for that.

The news he'd just received unsettled him, and he hadn't had time to accept it yet. The thought of his mom trapped under the earth in some horrendous jail cell in near darkness, grieving and worried about her family, unable to do anything but sit and be tormented by her thoughts and perhaps her captor's cruelness, was too much to bear. All those years. How could it be possible? He'd rather think of her as dead than tortured.

As soon as David had said the words Jay had feared, he'd told them he wanted to go home. "I understand you're upset, Jay," David had said. "But please at least consider helping us. Your mother needs us."

"Please don't say that," he'd told David, fighting back tears and hoping he wouldn't totally break down and bawl like a baby in front of this guy, who would definitely think he was a wuss if he did. "We don't know she is for sure." Something inside him wouldn't let him accept it. They had no proof.

"Just think about what we've talked about." David had laid a hand on his shoulder, and Jay had felt a jolt of electricity at his touch. "Listen to your heart."

Jay hadn't liked it one bit. He'd shrugged David off and muttered, "I just want to go. This is too weird."

"Hold on one sec." David had left the room and had returned with a long, shiny sword in a leather sheath lying in both hands.

"Wow, what's that?" It was impressive, he couldn't deny.

"This sword is very special," he'd informed him. "It's enchanted. I wanted you to see it before you leave."

The sword was beautiful. Its shiny, steel handle stuck out from the top of the sheath, shaped like a cross, complete with intricate designs accented with gold, and covered with many small, red, ruby-colored stones arranged in patterns glittering in the light. He had reached out and touched the handle, and a spark traveled through his body. He'd almost been too upset by the news of his possible imprisoned mother to take in how incredibly impressive it was, although he had whispered, "Sweet," for effect. "Who enchanted it?"

David had grinned like a man with a secret. "This sword was enchanted by the only one who has the power to do so. The queen."

"Wow."

"This sword is yours and you will train with it." David held it out proudly as Jay raised his eyebrows. "I mean, should you choose to join us, of course." It had seemed David was trying to be unintimidating. However, he couldn't mask his overwhelming force. Jay thought maybe he really didn't have a choice in the matter. "I'll keep it here for safekeeping."

Now Jay and Nina were walking back from Jay's encounter with the leader of the Unit army, Nina practically running to keep up with him. Everything about the situation left him unsettled. Suddenly, he felt he needed to know everything that had happened the night Nina had come across the queen. He stopped, causing Nina to do the same, turning to face her in the glow of the dim flashlight. "You mentioned when you let the queen go, she made a new tunnel. Can you show me?"

"What? I thought you wanted to go home."

"I want to see it."

"Okay," she agreed, appearing apprehensive. "But, why?"

"Something tells me it will help me understand."

"Understand what? Your mother?"

"Everything. To understand everything." He was desperate to see it, believing somehow when he did, he would know for sure if the queen was his mother or not.

"You sure about this?"

Her hesitance told him he was on to something. "Dead sure."

"All right, I know a shortcut. Follow me."

As they traveled upward to the main tunnel, the sounds of the street above them became louder. They passed Chompy, to whom Nina tossed a fresh enchanted piece of fruit. In her haste, she bonked it in the head with it, but it didn't appear to mind. They passed the part of the wall where Jay had left the X when he'd first stumbled into the tunnel system. The next intersecting passageway was about a hundred feet away and was the one Nina ventured into. Jay followed her, his flashlight lighting the path before them. The tunnel crossed into another path, this one smaller and crudely dug out. "This is it," she announced as they turned left.

The floor was an uneven mix of rocks and clay. Jay's legs burned after just a minute of slogging through it, his shoes sinking slightly with each step. Luckily, they didn't have far to go.

"Stop, Jay," Nina directed. "This is the end of the path and there's only one trap."

"Oh, man. I'm totally not in the mood for traps."

"Sorry, the Gray's made your mom put it here." She corrected herself when Jay flashed her a disapproving look. "I mean, the queen. It's not a big deal. Probably one of the easiest traps to solve." She bent down, examining the ground. "Shine your light here." She pointed, and he obeyed. "There it is. See that large rock?" It lay before them, roughly a square shape about four by four feet. Although covered in dirt, its outline was clear.

"Yes," he answered.

"We both have to land on it at the exact same time, okay?"

"Oh-kay," he said, uncertain.

"Stand right here and we'll both jump when I count to three." Jay maneuvered forward until he was side by side with her. "One, two, three." They took a huge leap and landed with a thud. The foundation teetered, similar to a raft floating on water. His right foot rolled on the small pebbles on its surface, and he was thankful he was able to stop himself before he fell. They each extended a hand toward the wall to regain their balance, then clasped onto each another.

Jay's chest felt tight, and he was having a difficult time catching his breath. "Whoa! Now what?" These traps really sucked, and he hated them more than anything.

"Now we jump and run at the same time. Follow me to the edge of the rock." Still holding onto each other, they crept to the edge as it tilted with their weight. "See the light ahead?" She pointed to a faint light in the darkness that indicated an exit, and he was glad for it. "I'll count again. Jump and run forward as fast as you can once we're off. Focus on the light and don't stop no matter what, understand?"

"Yeah."

At the count of three, they jumped and sprinted down the tunnel with all their strength. A mighty crash resounded behind them. Jay merely cringed and kept running while the ground seemed to crumble underneath his feet.

Needle-like pricks of pain attacked as pebbles sprayed his back and legs. Dirt filled his eyes and lungs. For a moment, he thought he would suffocate until the light appeared once more through the slits in his eyes. Desire for fresh oxygen motivated him to run faster still, despite the tunnel spinning around him.

After what seemed like several long minutes, they reached a dead end and Jay lifted his head, rubbing his eyes with the inside of his shirt to remove the irritants that had invaded them. The opening was a good ten feet up, and the soft glow of sunlight and cool fresh air beckoned him upward as dirt and dust continued to take over his lungs. They both doubled over, grabbing their knees and coughing like chronic chain smokers.

Jay turned to find a pair of hollow eyes observing him. Before he knew it, a scream had emerged from his throat as he backed up against the wall as far from it as possible while shining the now dirty flashlight on what had frightened him, wiping away the tears that helped flush his eyes. The floating dust glowed in the flashlight's beam, clouding his vision. Grit crunched between his teeth, dry and bitter.

"What? What is it?" Nina asked in a panic, waving the cloud away with both hands, still coughing.

Jay wiped clumps of dirt off the flashlight lens with his fingers. The beam brightened, revealing a dirty skull peering at them through the cloudy dust. Strands of black hair clung to a patch of skin in the center of the head, forming a grotesque sort of Mohawk. "What the..."

"Oh, yeah. You run into those sometimes," Nina said while dusting herself off.

"Someone d-died in here?"

"Looks like it."

Jay's heart thumped at an alarming rate. "Oh, man." He spit, unable to handle the taste and the sense of dirt in his mouth. He shined the light behind them, not wanting to see the skull anymore, and noticed the path had completely closed off. It seemed they were trapped inside a cave-in. "Great. How are you gonna get back?"

"It'll open again in about twenty minutes."

Relief filled him, thankful she'd be able to get out. Still, his heart did not slow, continuing to beat a million times a minute. "Not gonna lie, these traps are straight-up terrifying." He searched up, eager to get out.

"You get used to it." Nina's face and clothes were coated with filth. She looked like she had just crawled out of a hole after being buried alive.

"Yeah, not seeing that happening. How do we get up there?" He motioned up with his head and eyes.

"Do what I do." Nina used the rocks embedded in the sides of the hole to climb upward. They almost seemed placed there for that very purpose. She made it look easy, but Jay didn't have the same experience. By the time he struggled his way to the top, he was puffing with the effort.

When he pulled himself out of the earth, his heart stopped. "Whoa."

The sun was setting behind the mountain, washing everything in deep orange glow. The place felt oddly familiar. Thoughts came rushing to him of the night he, Brian and Thad had come to this very spot months ago. This time, however, he was seeing it all from a different viewpoint. This time, he was inside the charred remains of the old burnt up house. He took a slow look around, his throat dry as he swallowed a mouthful of gritty dust.

There wasn't much left—just warped beams, blackened wood, and piles of debris that had once been walls and furniture. A breeze stirred loose ashes into the air, and for a second, it looked like smoke rising again. He didn't know what he was looking for. Maybe a memory. Maybe nothing. But something about standing here made his chest tighten, like the house still held pieces of a story he wasn't ready to hear.

"What's wrong?" Nina asked.

"This," he told her in a voice just above a whisper, gazing straight ahead as Nina stared at him with concern, "was my house."

30

SON OF A QUEEN

He remembered seeing her months ago, rising from this very spot, her white clothes shining in the moonlight. She'd disappeared twelve years before and would only have been in her mid-thirties, yet her hair had been completely white. All this time, Jay had thought he'd seen an angel that night—that or a ghost. But it was his mother, his very much alive mother!

"I saw her," he told Nina, who merely responded with a look. "About eight months ago, Brian and Thad dared me to come up here with them. People say this place is haunted. They were trying to scare me, but they ended up being the ones running off and left me here alone."

"Weren't you afraid?"

"Terrified. I would've run too, but I couldn't move. She screamed when she saw this." He motioned around him. "It must've killed her inside."

"Her hair turned white," Nina said. Jay noticed a tear slip from her right eye, catching the last streak of sunlight as it traced down her cheek. "I saw it happen that night, like... something left her. Her spirit, her hope—just gone."

"You were there?" Jay asked and Nina nodded. He remembered hearing a young child's voice that night, but he hadn't seen her. He sat down on the edge of the once beautiful hardwood floor, his feet dangling into the hole from where they'd come. "She thinks we're dead."

Nina joined him in silence, her large blue eyes standing out even more against her dark, dirt-smeared skin. She looked at him with a sad, empathetic expression, and for a moment, Jay felt the weight of her unspoken understanding. She scanned around at the charred remains. "The Grays must have set the house on fire after they captured her so many years ago."

"I'm sure she assumed we died in this fire. That had to have been the first time she'd seen this house since those things took her like twelve years ago." Jay couldn't imagine what she must have felt—to realize her family had been burnt in the blaze. His heart felt heavy, weighed down with a sorrow that seemed to settle deep within him. "And the Grays probably believe our whole family died. But I spent the night at Aunt Vicki's when they did this."

"How did your dad escape?"

"I don't know. He just... he just didn't die." But in a way, he kind of did. He was never the same after losing her. Jay swallowed the lump in his throat. Yet it remained. "Has anyone told her you found me?"

"We haven't seen her since. We haven't been able to locate her."

"In the jail?"

"They moved her."

Jay pulled his necklace out of his shirt and held onto the ring. "And this—why did she leave it behind?"

"It's a Paragon, Jay."

"Paragon?"

"Yes, people say her powers come from it."

"Her powers?" He examined it. It looked like a normal ruby ring to him. How could a ring possess a power like that? "How?"

"No one knows. She used it to enchant the traps."

"She gave me her power?"

"David said she has another Paragon."

"Another one?"

"He said she used it to enchant some things without the Grays knowing before they moved her. She enchanted the swords, the crocodile fruit, the coin—"

"Your collar?"

"No. David told me Vicki did that."

"Aunt Vicki?" Jay couldn't believe what he was hearing. Aunt Vicki also had a ring. She'd always said they were gifts from his grandparents who died before he was born. Was that all a lie? "Aunt Vicki has powers?"

"I know she can heal. Beyond that and what she did to the collar, I'm not sure."

"So that's how she healed you." It was all making some kind of sense now.

"Yeah."

"Is Aunt Vicki from the Underground too?"

"She is. Your mom helped her escape. The Grays wanted to kill her."

Jay remembered Aunt Vicki saying that his mom had saved her from some bad people. The Grays were the bad people! "This is unreal."

"But you still can't tell her you know about the Underground. Not yet."

Jay nodded, biting his lower lip. "Aunt Vicki would be ecstatic if she knew Mom was alive. And Dad. Oh my gosh—Dad would lose his mind!"

"Really, Jay. It's important. Not until David says it's time."

"I won't. I promise." Keeping the secret was the least of his concerns right now. He felt unable to process all that had been thrown at him. "This is all so hard to believe." His mother was alive? She had powers? Aunt Vicki too? It was overwhelming. "And all this comes from this stone?" Jay admired it with awe.

"Yes. And your mom, the queen, she must have left it behind for you."

"Why would she do that?" It didn't give him powers, did it? He wondered.

Nina shrugged. "Maybe there's something you're supposed to do with it."

"Like what?" But Nina didn't answer. She might have shrugged again. Jay wasn't looking at her. His attention was drawn to the hole in the charred wooden floor. On a black, jagged piece of wood hung a piece of fabric that looked as if it might have been brilliant white at one time, but now was stained and gray with age. Somehow, he knew it had belonged to his mother—a remnant of what she'd worn the night he'd seen her. He reached down and freed the cloth and held it close to his heart.

There *was* something he was supposed to do. He had no idea what, but whatever it was, it burned in his heart with ferocity.

"If she's still alive, Jay, we'll find her. We have to."

He glanced down at the fabric as he stroked it with dirty fingers, coating it with filth. "She's alive. I know it."

Reflecting on how unjustly his mother had been imprisoned for so long, and all the years he'd spent without her, a surge of fury welled up inside him. Those Gray, mutant freaks had taken her from him and Dad. What right did they have to do that? They'd stolen her and burned down their home. He had never felt such intense hate before. It rose from a deep part of his soul that he hadn't known existed, growing like an entity all its own.

"So, you'll help us?" Nina's voice was soft, as if afraid of the answer.

Never was he so sure about anything in his life. He needed to free his mother from her dark, tortuous prison. She'd suffered for far too long. It was his duty, no matter what, to do this for her. He had to. She was a queen, and he was her son. He was the son of a queen!

"Sorry. I know you need time to think about it." Nina bowed her head, seeming disappointed, yet under-standing.

Jay laid his hand on Nina's, and she lifted her gaze, her eyes now wet. Clean stripes from her tears lined her dirty face. "I don't need time." Nina's eyes brightened. "I want to help my mother He wrapped the cloth around his left wrist three times, then tucked the loose end under the last wrap to secure it. With that, he pushed himself to his feet, standing tall on the broken, charred floorboards. Dirty from head to toe, he flipped his cap backwards on his head, feeling like a warrior with the queen's powerful ring on his neck. He was sure he'd never felt more ready than at that moment and he would feel even more so once he was in possession of his enchanted sword. He was ready to fight—or at least to train.

He had no clue what was in store, or of what dangers lie ahead, but there was one thing he was certain of. "Let's do it," he declared. "Let's save the queen."

ABOUT THE AUTHOR

Whitney J. Cogle has been a story-teller most of her life, starting with puppet plays written and performed as a teenager. Her passion for adventure followed her into adulthood and can be found in the pages of the Paragon series along with many more adventures to come.

Whitney lives in Colorado with her husband, two daughters and crazy, energetic shih tzu, Mojo.

To read more about Whitney and her books, please visit her website: www.WhitneyJCogle.com or www.Mocha Frog.com.

BOOK TWO

Paragon

The Vindicators

Whitney J. Cogle

PROLOGUE
THE CREATOR AND THE CREATED

"Father," the created one uttered, the word echoing in the dark, dreary room made of rock. The air was frigid enough to chill the bone. The Grays liked it cold.

An old Gray sat behind a stone desk. "Do not call me that, Makk. I have told you not to call me that." His small mouth pursed together, leaving many vertical lines around the slit in his sagging face. Most of the Grays had teardrop-shaped faces, but this one was so old his face had grown into a long, misshapen form.

"Sorry, King. I've done all you've asked."

The Gray king placed his long-fingered hands on the surface in front of him. As with his face, they too had a lot of extra skin, the knuckles like balls shoved underneath it all. "Good. There is still more to do. It is our duty to change the prophecy. Do you understand, Creation?"

He nodded. This Gray was his father, although not in the natural sense. Years ago, the government had created Makk, and according to the Gray standing before him, they had fashioned him for a purpose. At one time, he had been special.

"We must prove the Unit, Mary, wrong." He clenched his old hand and punched the air. "It is necessary to follow the plan exactly. Why are you holding your head down?"

Makk hadn't wanted to turn on the others, especially the queen, but he'd had no choice. The king had threatened to destroy him after a Unit discovered him hiding out in the tunnels. Only seconds before Makk's death, he'd offered information that had saved him. Maybe it made him a coward, maybe a traitor, but it also kept him alive. Besides, he had a plan. "It's just that, some of them are my friends."

"Friends?" The old Gray leaned forward. "Stop acting like you have emotions when you do not. Do you hear me?" He slammed his long-fingered hand upon the desktop. "If you are any relation to me, you do not have these emotions." He leaned back. "You cannot." He studied Makk with a critical eye. "Perhaps I should have destroyed you a long time ago. I should not have permitted the rejected creations from Rend's experiments to live."

Makk did not respond in word or action. If he were to beg for his life when the king lamented about his existence, as he often did, it would only satiate the king's thirst for control.

"I believed the experiments might be of use someday and I thought I had been correct. At least about two of you."

"You *were* correct, King. I will do nothing to displease you."

"That would be a wise decision. Do not frustrate me like the girl, Viki, has done. I knew leaving her in the tunnel system had been a mistake as soon as she turned on me. I had to kill her—to have Rend kill her. Do not become my enemy or you will suffer the same fate."

Viki had escaped years ago and had changed the spelling of her name by adding another letter. Makk assumed because going by the four letters given to her by the Grays was a reminder of her life in the Underground. "I won't." Viki wasn't dead. However, Makk would never discredit the king by saying so. He could sense her Paragon sometimes when she used it. The magic tied the three Paragons together through the Adoremus Stone. It was the Paragon that had spared her and the Paragon that gave her away.

The king was silent for a moment as he eased back into his chair. "I dislike the way you are looking at me." He scrunched his face. "You are weak. Pathetic! You must be strong, not weak. You will never complete this task if you remain the wretched mush that you are."

"I'm sorry..."

"Stop saying you are sorry. This mission is vital. Do you not understand it?"

"I do."

"We must stop this prophecy! Although Rend had begged me to spare your life, there was a time I believed you all to be unimportant, less than nothing." He leaned in to stress his point. "You have proven to be the most important of them all." He pointed at Makk with a long finger. "You are the key."

Makk knew better than to let what he thought might be a compliment from his creator affect him. For, as quickly as he spoke something resembling kindness, he would turn around and say something cruel. Grays didn't seem to possess any emotions outside of anger. Perhaps the Gray in him wouldn't allow the good feelings to come.

"As much as I hate this dreaded prophecy, it is essential to follow it and defeat the traitors that desire to destroy us and our civilization," the old king continued. "Mary was right on every occasion. Never once had I heard her foretell something that did not happen just the way she predicted. We kept her alive because of her usefulness until she uttered this prophecy against us." He pounded his fist into his wrinkled palm. "She spoke of this horrific incident, and she was happy for it. Curse her grave! We were correct in disposing of her. There will be no more evil prophecies against us now."

"No, my king. But I'm confused. We must follow the prophecy to stop the prophecy?"

"Must I continue to explain? The prophecy says, 'together you will overcome or together fall apart.' This can only mean that we need to get those in the prophecy together and destroy them all. Our army is more than capable. Your job is to find them and bring them to me. Do you think there is any way you might stop being completely worthless and do that?"

"Whatever you wish," Makk said, nodding.

"I hope you are strong enough."

The king thought Makk might have too much Unit emotion in him, and he himself was unsure. He was told he didn't have emotions, but he did feel some things. Like a feeling toward David for being taken by Rend to train the Gray army and toward Viki for going off to live on the outside that he thought might be jealousy. A feeling toward the king that might be guilt. And a feeling for the queen he thought might be love. As much as he tried to ignore these emotions and say he didn't feel them, they were there. The Paragon had birthed them and wouldn't release him no matter what he did to push them away. The crazy thing was, they seemed to grow in strength as time went on.

"I am," he said. His brother and sister had left him to rot and die alone. Why should he care about them at all? And the queen? Well, she never tried to save him, and with all her power, surely, she could have. Why had she chosen to free Viki and not him? And yet he still cherished her. But he had to save himself. And this was the only way.

The king regarded him with agitation. "Now, because of you, we are aware of this secret army forming. We know this prophecy is developing. I cannot go deep within the tunnel system as you can, so I need you to be my eyes and ears. We need to find all the Units involved. The only one we have now is Tara. We need to find the others before destroying her."

Makk shifted where he stood at the sound of the queen's name. Makk hadn't called her Tara since he found out she was the queen, and the king hadn't called her queen since she had deserted him.

"Every group has a leader," the kind continued. "Once we locate this leader, we can get them all together. You need to find him. All you have to do," he growled with something resembling a smile forming on his small mouth, "is bring him to me. I want him alive, understand? You must befriend him."

"Understood."

"Whatever you must do, find him so we can destroy this group and end their rebellion once and for all."

Makk was silent.

The old Gray squinted and looked deep into Makk's eyes. Makk wanted to turn away from them, as they were so dark, so fierce, it seemed he was peering into the essence of pure evil. "And bring Rend to me also if you can locate him. If he is still alive."

Rend had disappeared after Makk had ratted on him. Mark agreed to the king's request, although he wasn't sure he'd be able to do it when the time came.

"Now go fulfill your obligation. Bring all in the prophecy to me, and you shall have anything you ask."

"Yes, my king."

"Anything you wish."

Makk allowed himself to smile, but not too much. He thought of the queen and knew what he would ask for.

ALSO BY WHITNEY J COGLE

A war is brewing under the earth...

Paragon - The Vindicators

Jay Matthews might be the missing piece to the puzzle, David, the leader of the underground Unit army called the Vindicators, has been searching for. Should Jay decide to join them, he will become the Swordsman in the prophecy and will help lead the Units to victory over the Grays who have mastered them for so long.

The Units aren't the only ones who have something to lose in this battle. The Grays are not only dangerous to the Units underground, but also to the humans that live on its surface. David and Jay must work together to defeat them.

But David has a dark secret, as does Jay's Aunt Vicki. Once Jay discovers them, his life will never be the same and will determine not only the future of the Underground, but also the world.

Book two in the thrilling Paragon series!

Now on the run from the Grays...

Paragon - The Half Breeds

With the Grays' stolen book in hand, Jay and his friends find themselves hiding out in the Colorado mountains beyond Brookfield as a strange family takes them in. David, their leader, is gone, and they are lost. Jay must step up and lead them, although he is reluctant to do so, and some refuse to follow.

Their battle against the Grays is just beyond the horizon. Together, this band of teens will train to fight while discovering how to tap into the power of the Paragon just as Jay's mother, Tara, his Aunt Vicki and Old Mary had years before they were born.

But time is running out. The Grays are closing in, sending half-breeds to scout the area in search of them. Even though Jay and his friends have only just begun to train, they must now make a choice—to run again or face their fears, ready or not. If they don't, the Grays and their half-breeds will make it for them.

Book three in the gripping Paragon Series!

The time has come to fight...

Paragon - The Gray King

As Jay, Nina and the Vindicators have been striving to free those below ground and to save those above it, the Gray king has devised a plan of his own. Now under Jay's leadership, it's up to the Vindicators to stop it. This is what they've been training for.

It won't be easy. Many obstacles will come their way, including a half-breed army, deadly traps and even traitors among them. Making it more difficult, Jay's family has become involved and he must make sure they come out alive. The Paragon is the key. If Jay and the other leaders of the Vindicators can tap into its power, they may win, but only if they figure out how to beat all odds and stop the Gray king's deadly scheme.

In this underground journey, full of creatures that want to eradicate them, a prophecy they'll need to decipher to survive, and the Paragon they must learn to master, this group of teens and adults find their biggest obstacle is something they didn't expect. Time. And it's growing short.

Book four in the electrifying Paragon series!

The end has come...

Paragon - The Adoremus Stone

As Old Mary's prophecy begins to unfold, Jay, Nina and the other members of the prophecy are faced with a fierce battle against Grays under the earth. They now have all the members of the prophecy together, but the prophecy must be fulfilled in its entirety or all humanity will be lost forever.

It's not just the Grays they must overcome. The Grays have bred an army of half-human, half-Gray creatures, and have created a weapon designed to destroy the world using a piece of their planet that holds an unusual energy—the Adoremus Stone.

These few humans, together with the hundreds of Units in the Vindicator army, must battle against a horde of millions of half-breeds and Grays to keep them from using the Adoremus Stone to destroy life on Earth. Although vastly outnumbered, they have the Paragon in their possession. Yet, to defeat the Grays and their army, they must work as a team to uncover the Paragon's true power.

Book five - the final book in the exhilarating Paragon series!

www.ingramcontent.com/pod-product-compliance
Lightning Source LLC
Chambersburg PA
CBHW021220250626
47155CB00008B/2897